SHERLOCK HOLMES

THE SOLDIER'S DAUGHTER AND
OTHER STORIES

Sherlock Holmes

The Soldier's Daughter
and other stories

BY

JOHN H. WATSON MD
LATE OF THE ARMY MEDICAL DEPARTMENT

Published by the author
malcolm.knott999@gmail.com

© Malcolm Knott 2017
The author asserts the moral right to be
identified as the author of this work.
ISBN-13: 978-1542597050
Printed and bound by Create Space

Set in Garamond 11.5 pt

CONTENTS

THE SOLDIER'S DAUGHTER

IN the summer of 1885 I had been sharing rooms with my friend Mr Sherlock Holmes for about three years and we had settled into a comfortable existence together.

One morning, not long after the painstaking investigation which had culminated in the arrest of Butterfield the Margate poisoner and his deplorable nephew, we sat reading the newspapers over a late breakfast. The bell rang and an engraved card was sent up. It announced Miss Violet Dungate, of 87 Welbeck Street, and was followed a few moments later by the lady herself. She was in her middle twenties, quietly but fashionably dressed, with delicate hands and a fresh open face partly concealed behind a small veil. She was clearly in a state of some agitation.

'Miss Dungate,' said Holmes, as he waved her to the armchair, 'This is my friend and colleague, Doctor Watson, before whom you may speak quite freely. Pray tell us how we can help you.'

'Mr Holmes, I am so desperately worried, I hardly know where to begin or how to collect my thoughts.'

'You must begin at the beginning. At the moment I know nothing about you, beyond the obvious facts that your father is a soldier, your mother died some years ago and you have recently ceased to play the violin.'

Our visitor was plainly taken aback and somewhat

flustered by this exhibition of my friend's powers.

'My dear Holmes,' I said, 'you must not alarm the young lady in this way. Explain yourself, and put her mind at rest.'

'It is really very simple, Miss Dungate. When I see that your dainty boots are polished to a high gloss, even under the instep, I readily infer that you live in a military household. Your mourning ring is well worn, and suggests the loss of the other parent some years ago. The fingertips of your left hand, like my own, show the slight hardening characteristic of the violinist, and the dark shadows under your eyes, which you have been at pains to conceal with your veil, tell me that the last few days have been too full of care for you to practice your music.'

'Mr Holmes this is really quite remarkable and you are perfectly correct in all that you say.' She took a moment to compose herself and then continued. 'I have been recommended to consult you by my cousin Penelope Mortimer, who tells me that your powers are formidable, and in my present anxiety I should be more than grateful for your help.

'I must tell you that my father is Lieutenant-Colonel George Dungate, late of the Royal Fusiliers. He retired from the Army after my mother's last illness and we have our own house in Welbeck Street. We keep a cook-house-keeper, a maid-of-all-work and my father's manservant, Stannard, who has been with us for some years. All three servants are of excellent character.

'On Thursday of last week we had a small dinner party. Besides my father and myself the guests were my father's sister Mrs Mortimer, her husband, and their daughter – my cousin Penelope, whom I have just mentioned. She is the same age as myself. The other member of the party was a Mr Wilmott. He was a single gentleman of about my father's age. Neither I nor my father had met him before. I understand he had recently had some business dealings with my uncle, and I believe he was invited to make up the party at my uncle's suggestion. Mr Wilmott had recently moved into Devonshire Place, so he was to be our neighbour.

'The evening went well enough, as my cousin and I have always plenty to talk about, and my aunt has the trick of putting people at their ease. However, I did not much take to Mr Wilmott, whom I thought a little loud and conceited. After dinner we ladies retired to the drawing room and few minutes later the gentlemen joined us. I thought then a change had come over my father. He seemed very quiet and withdrawn. In fact after a few minutes he said he was not feeling very well and thought that he should not be very late to bed. My aunt and uncle took the hint and the party broke up shortly before midnight. We said our farewells and the guests departed.

'I expected my father would retire at once but to my surprise he showed no inclination to do so and on the contrary returned to the drawing room with a glass of brandy. I sat with him, and we talked together quietly for an hour or so and possibly longer. I asked him if all was well and he made some answer which put my mind at rest. Then we spoke briefly about our plans for the following day, and made our way to bed.

'The following morning I was woken by Mrs Finch, the housekeeper, to tell me that my father was not in the house and his bed had not been slept in. I got up at once and stepped into my dressing room, where I found this note on the table.'

She handed the note to Holmes who studied it carefully for a moment or two and then handed it to me. It read—

My Dear Violet,
I have had to go away suddenly. Do not alarm yourself. I am quite well. I have taken your mother's pendant.
Your affectionate Father

'The pendant in question, Mr Holmes, contains a single large emerald in a silver mount. I believe it is quite valuable and it is certainly the most precious piece of jewellery I own. I was not wearing it that night and indeed I have worn it on very few occasions. Nothing else was taken and my father left no word of his destination, or his reason for leaving so suddenly.'

'Forgive me Miss Dungate,' asked Holmes. 'is your father in any financial embarrassment?'

'I do not believe so. We are not rich, but we are in comfortable circumstances and my father has never been an extravagant man. I cannot think why he should have taken my pendant.'

'Has your father done anything of this sort before?'

'Never.'

'Were you on good terms with him?'

'Yes. My father is a rather private man, perhaps more so since my mother's death, but we are very dear to each other.'

'I interrupted you – please continue.'

'Worse was to come. No sooner had I discovered the pendant missing than I learned that there had been a tragedy in the night. Mr Wilmott had been bludgeoned to death in the street. He had been found shortly before midnight, evidently a few minutes after he left our house.'

'Ah yes,' said Holmes, 'I recall reading something of the case – a very commonplace and unremarkable crime. But what has this to do with your father? Had he left the house at any time during the evening?'

'No, Mr Holmes. I can swear that he was never out of my sight until I went to bed shortly after one o'clock in the morning. When I learned what had happened I went at once to my uncle's house but he knew nothing of it. When the party broke up Stannard had summoned a four wheeler for my uncle and his family, and they had offered to drop Mr Wilmott off at his house. But he said it was only a short distance and had set off to walk in the opposite direction. That was the last time my uncle had seen him alive.

'I then made enquiries at my father's club, the Army

and Navy, but they had seen nothing of him for the last day or so, and knew of nothing amiss.

'That afternoon the police called; an Inspector Hopkins from Scotland Yard.'

Holmes and I exchanged glances, for we both knew Stanley Hopkins as one of the smarter Scotland Yard detectives who had more than once sought Holmes's advice in cases of particular difficulty.

'They had found my father's address in Mr Wilmott's pocket book. I assured the Inspector I could throw no light on the mystery, and told him of my father's disappearance. Of course his suspicions were aroused but it is quite impossible that my father should have been connected with this horrible murder, and besides he has not an enemy in the world.

'This was a week ago, and since then I have heard not a word from my father. Please tell me what is to be done. I am at my wits' end. Shall I ever see him again?'

'Come come,' I said, leaning forward and putting my hand on her shoulder, 'we must not despair. Your father's own note says that you are not to alarm yourself, and you must not do so.'

Just then there was a knock at the door and Mrs Hudson announced a second visitor – none other than Stanley Hopkins himself. A large well-built man with a cheerful countenance, he stepped briskly into the room.

'Why Miss Dungate,' he said, as he caught sight of her, 'I fancy we are here on the same business. I take it you have told Mr Holmes everything you know?'

'I have,' she replied, looking at him candidly, 'I hope he may be able to explain my father's sudden disappearance.'

'Why then, Mr Holmes,' said Hopkins, as he was motioned to the vacant chair, 'You are already acquainted with the facts of the case. I must tell you frankly that so far we have made very little headway, and would welcome any help that you can give us.

'Of course,' he continued, 'there is no direct evidence to link the Colonel's disappearance with the attack on Mr Wilmott, but it does seem to be a very strange coincidence, and I believe the Colonel had something to fear. Why else should he leave so suddenly in the middle of the night? We know he took Miss Dungate's emerald but he was evidently not short of money. I have since learned that the following morning he called into Drummond's Bank in Trafalgar Square and cashed a cheque for £100. Since then he seems to have vanished from the face of the earth.

'As to Wilmott, my first thought was that he had died at the hands of a drunken ruffian or footpad. But robbery could not have been the motive, for the man had on him a gold watch and chain and a small case of sovereigns, neither of which had been taken.'

'Perhaps the robber was surprised before he could finish his work,' I suggested.

'That is one possibility,' said Hopkins, 'but no witness

to the attack has yet come forward.'

'Who discovered the body?' asked Holmes.

'One of my officers on night beat, a steady young constable, and very alert. It was shortly after midnight and must have been within a few minutes of the assault. He found Wilmott sprawled in the gutter with his heavy stick beside him, no more than a hundred yards from the Colonel's house. He was not yet dead – and here is another curious feature of the case, which so far we have kept out of the newspapers. My constable knelt down beside the man who groaned and murmured a few words. He said "The blankets – it was the blankets."

Holmes leaned forward, with a glint in his eye and an expression of the keenest interest on his face.

'Are you sure of those words?'

'I have questioned my man very closely and he says there can be no mistake. Those were the only words Wilmott uttered. Soon afterwards he lost consciousness and expired.'

'Do these words mean anything to you Miss Dungate?' asked Holmes.

'Nothing at all Mr Holmes' she replied. 'I am quite at a loss, I assure you.'

'Wilmott's injuries' Hopkins continued, 'show that he had been felled by a single blow from his own stick. The stick itself was a valuable item, but again, that had not been taken. Beyond that we have no information. I have spoken to the servants, of course, and I have seen Miss Dungate's uncle and aunt, but like her they can throw no light on the mystery.'

'What can you tell me about the dead man?' asked Holmes.

'Not a great deal is known,' said Hopkins. 'He had only recently moved to this district and for some years past had lived in Museum Street, near your old rooms, Mr Holmes. He was a private banker or moneylender with no family of his own and pretty close about his business. However he had his finger in a great many pies, and I should not be surprised if he had made one or two enemies over the years.'

'Well, Hopkins,' said Sherlock Holmes, 'This case is not without its interesting features, and to oblige Miss Dungate and yourself I should be very happy to look into it. Miss Dungate, the weather is very pleasant and Welbeck Street is but a short distance. I suggest Dr Watson and I take a stroll and visit you this afternoon. Shall we say three o'clock? In the meantime please try not to distress yourself further. I have no reason to believe your father is in danger.'

I knew from long experience that Holmes would not be willing to confide his thoughts at such an early stage of the investigation, for it was an axiom of his that all the relevant facts must be assembled before any attempt is made to formulate a theory. In any case I had a luncheon appointment of my own at the Holborn Restaurant. However shortly before the appointed hour I returned to Baker Street and we set off together. It was a glorious day, and the dust from the road and the sun beating down on the paving stones made me wish that I was out of town, striding through the green shade of the New Forest and breathing the bracing air of Hampshire.

Before long we turned into New Cavendish Street and arrived at the corner of Welbeck Street.

'This I fancy', said Holmes, 'is where poor Wilmott met his untimely death. Of course after seven days and a shower or two there is nothing to be seen – if only they had consulted me at the time something might have been done.'

He glanced about him. The streets were wide and straight and there was a clear view in each direction. But this part of London is still very quiet, for the most part comprising the homes of professional gentlemen and private families, and even in the middle of the afternoon there was only the occasional pedestrian going about his business.

We turned into Welbeck Street and soon found the Colonel's house, a tall narrow, terraced property, of a type familiar in Bloomsbury and Marylebone, which had probably stood for two or three generations. It was clean and smart, and in excellent repair, with only a small window box at one of the upper windows to show the softening influence of the daughter of the house.

The door was opened by Stannard, the manservant, a tall well-built man in his late forties whose large hands and weather-beaten face suggested that he had not always worn a servant's livery. He showed us into the drawing room where we were met by Miss Dungate. She was still very nervous, if a little less flustered than she had been earlier in the day.

'Now,' said Holmes, 'I apologise for the intrusion but I must ask you to show us over the entire house, including the servants' quarters.'

'Of course,' said Miss Dungate, and led the way.

We inspected the dining room where the party had eaten and the drawing room to which the ladies had retired.

'And is this,' asked Holmes, 'where you and your father sat on the night of his disappearance?'

'Yes indeed, and the room was exactly as you see it. Nothing has been changed.'

'There is a large window I see,' said Holmes 'but this is at the back of the house. There is no view from here of Welbeck Street?'

'None at all, and on that evening the curtains were drawn.'

'Is there a rear entrance to the house?'

'Yes, through here,' she said, leading the way, 'There is a door into the small walled garden. The door in the garden wall leads through to the mews at the rear. As we keep no carriage that door is hardly ever used and we keep it padlocked.'

'Most interesting,' Holmes said. 'May I ask you to fetch the key?'

She did so, and a moment later we passed through the door and into the mews, which was deserted except for a large cat sunning himself on the cobbles. In a moment

Holmes had dropped to his knees like a bloodhound on the scent and was minutely examining the lower part of the wall. After a minute or two, with my help, he clambered up and examined the brickwork at the top of the wall with the same intensity. Then he dropped to the ground and with a grave expression on his face put his finger to his lips to enjoin us to silence.

We returned to the house and went upstairs to Miss Dungate's bedroom, where I noticed her violin case and music stand, and from there to the small dressing room next door.

'As you see, Mr Holmes,' she said, 'my dressing room is accessible from my bedroom and also from this corridor. It would not have been difficult for my father to enter quietly and take my pendant without disturbing me. This (indicating the dressing table) is where I found his note.'

We were then introduced to the housekeeper, Mrs Finch, who showed us her large upper room at the front of the house. This was comfortably furnished, and made homely by numerous fairings and trinkets accumulated in a lifetime of domestic service. The poor woman was clearly unsettled by our visit and the events of the last few days and I was grateful that Holmes only lingered for a moment or two. The maid, we were told, did not live in, but had lodgings over a haberdashers in Marylebone High Street to which she returned every evening when her duties were done.

The manservant then showed us his room, to the rear

of the house. This was a little smaller than the house-keeper's but remarkably neat and trim. Holmes looked about him with a quick eye and noticed an embroidered badge framed above the mantelpiece.

'You were in a line regiment I see,' he remarked.

'Yes sir,' replied Stannard, briskly enough, but with perhaps a moment's hesitation.

He seemed disposed to say no more, but took us down to the kitchen where we re-joined the housekeeper and the young maid. All three servants appeared to be sober and respectful. Holmes questioned them about the night of the Colonel's disappearance, and their accounts agreed with what Miss Dungate had already told us. The housekeeper and the maid were somewhat agitated but Stannard was of sterner stuff He repeated that the Colonel and his daughter had sat up until at least one o'clock in the morning and probably later, up to which time neither of them had left the house for even a moment. As to the Colonel's disappearance, he stoutly affirmed that his master would return in a few days and that the whole unfortunate business would soon blow over.

'I have no doubt, gentlemen,' he said, 'that he has gone away on some private business of his own which we are not to know about, but it will all come right very shortly.'

'Let us hope you are right,' said Holmes. 'By the way Stannard, which papers do you take in the house?'

'*The Morning Post*, Sir, and the *United Services Gazette*.'

'Excellent! And now Watson, I think we can return to

the drawing room where I have no doubt Miss Dungate is waiting to hear our news.'

Miss Dungate was indeed waiting for us, and she rose as we entered.

'Mr Holmes,' she asked 'Have you been able to throw any light on the matter?'

'I have,' said Holmes. 'Indeed, except for one or two trifling details I have been able to reconstruct the events of last Thursday evening in their entirety. However I am not yet ready to disclose my findings, and I imagine your first concern is to have your father home again safe and well?'

'Yes, Mr Holmes, that is my dearest wish.'

'I have no doubt that he will return in due time but I take it you would wish to hasten his arrival, if that could be managed?'

'Of course.'

'Then may I suggest you insert the following advertisement in tomorrow's edition of the Morning Post. Mind, you must do this yourself, and no one else must know of it. Do you understand?'

'Yes of course, I will do as you ask.'

Holmes then handed her a scrap of paper on which he had written—

Violet. Apologies for sudden departure. All well. I am coming home early next week. Father

For a moment Miss Dungate looked troubled.

'Do you say this will bring my father home, Mr

Holmes?'

'I have no doubt of it – and I think it may have other consequences too, but nothing that will occasion you more than a trifling inconvenience.'

Then as we turned to take our leave he asked, 'By the way Miss Dungate, what was Stannard's regiment?'

'He was a recruiting sergeant in the 57th Foot – that was also my father's regiment before he exchanged into the Royal Fusiliers. I believe that was where they first met.'

'Thank you', said Holmes, 'That is exactly what I had supposed.'

Miss Dungate promised to alert us as soon as there was any further news, and a moment later we were on our way back to Baker Street.

'What do you make of it Watson?' asked Holmes when we were settled back in our own room.

'I am very much afraid,' I said, 'that there may be some financial scandal in the offing. We do not know when the emerald was taken. It may have been some days before the Colonel's departure. He was clearly uneasy on the night in question, which suggests that he had already made plans to go secretly away. But I cannot think that this has any connection with Wilmott's murder, which must surely be an unhappy coincidence.'

'And what of the dying man's reference to "blankets", do you not find that curious?'

'Not in the least. The man had received a fatal blow to the head and was probably delirious, his speech wandering and incoherent. Such cases are not uncommon from even a slight blow to the head. We should attach no particular importance to those words.'

'Well,' said Holmes thoughtfully, 'you may be right. It is certainly one of the more puzzling features of the case. However there is nothing more to be done for the next few days, so we can only wait upon events.'

News came rather sooner than I had expected. A few days later I returned from an afternoon call to find Holmes standing at the window with an air of unmistakable triumph.

'Ah Watson!' said he, You come hard on the heels of Stanley Hopkins, who is quite beside himself and threatens to have both of us taken up on a warrant for misprision of felony. My dear fellow,' he added, seeing my expression, 'pray don't alarm yourself. It is all bluster and he is quite powerless in the matter. One bird has flown and the other has returned to the nest. Here, read this.'

He handed me a short note in Miss Dungate's neat and legible hand—

> *Welbeck Street, Wednesday*
> *Dear Mr Holmes,*
>
> *I am pleased to tell you that my father returned home safely last night. He had been staying in the West Country for a few days, and there was, as you advised me, no cause for alarm. I do not think we need discuss the case any further and I know I can rely on your discretion in what turned out*

to be purely a family matter. I hope the enclosed cheque will
be sufficient to cover your professional fee.
  Yours truly, Violet Dungate
  PS. My pendant is quite safe.

'Well,' I said, 'this is welcome news indeed, although it seems to throw no more light on the death of Wilmott. But why is Hopkins so put out?'

'Ha!' cried Holmes, and with a flourish produced a second letter from the pocket of his dressing gown. This was much longer, and closely written on several sheets of paper in a painstaking hand, by a correspondent for whom this had clearly been a laborious task. It had been posted in Dover some two days earlier and read as follows—

Dear Mr Holmes,

By the time you read this I shall be on the high seas, having said farewell to old England for ever. I am not a young man but I shall try to make a new life, though it can be never so good as the old life which I cast away in a moment of anger. I owe it to you, Mr Holmes, and to myself, to set down what happened, and I shall do so now, as best I can.

I was only sixteen when I ran away from the unhappy place which was the only home I had ever known. I was a big strapping young fellow (no thanks to those who had me in their care) and there was talk of the Army going out East, so I came down to London, added a couple of years to my age and took the Queen's shilling in a public house near Trafalgar Square. The 57th West Middlesex was my regiment, known as the Die-Hards, with yellow collars and cuffs and a shilling a day which was more money than I had ever seen in my life. We were stationed at Hounslow, where I had some drill knocked into me, and sure enough within a few weeks we embarked for Constantinople and the Crimea.

You have heard of the great battles we fought, I am sure, and we did well enough at first, though a lot of men went down with cholera. But our generals got the slows and before long we were stuck fast in the trenches before Sevastopol and waiting for winter. What a winter that was! Thirty years have passed, but I shall never forget the cruel hardships we endured. Our fine uniforms soon went to pieces, and night after night we turned out in the driving snow and the biting wind, wet through to the skin and limping along like so many scarecrows with a few rags wrapped round our feet and our fingers numb with the pain; and then back to camp at dawn with nothing to eat but cold gruel and green coffee and no hope of anything better for weeks to come. I was a strong lad and I managed to hold on but many of my comrades died, or were sent home mutilated by the frostbite. We were so short of warm clothing it was for-bidden to bury a man in his blanket and in our battalion, if they heard of such a thing, they made us dig the man up again and strip the blanket from him.

The country was open, like a high heath, and only one road to speak of. This went down to the little harbour at

Balaclava where we landed our stores. There the whole of the Black Sea fleet was jammed into a little creek no bigger than a Cornish fishing village. What a filthy place that was, swarming with Turks and Tartars and all manner of human flotsam and jetsam! The road down to it was about six miles, steep and broken all the way, with not a horse or a mule to be found that was strong enough to pull a wagon. It would take a man the best part of a day to stumble down to the harbour and climb back up again and many a man was too weak to undertake the journey.

Now we had an officer, Captain Dungate as he was then, who was not much older than myself, though of course he came from a very good family. He was well thought of by the men and, as I believe, by his fellow officers also. He was my company officer so I saw something of him every day, and came to a good opinion of him for he shared our hardships and spared no pains to make things better for us when he could. One night when we were huddled down in the trenches Captain Dungate comes across to me and says, 'You're a strong man, Stannard. Will you come down to the harbour tomorrow to get some more blankets?'

Of course I said I would, though I knew it would mean a day and a night without sleep, for we should be back in the trenches again tomorrow. Then he told off a sergeant, and eight or nine other men, and soon after dawn we set off.

We had chosen a bad day, Mr Holmes, for it soon

began to snow again, and the sergeant went lame and had to fall out. We did our best to keep cheerful and trudged off down the hill but if truth be told we were tired and hungry, soaking wet, and half exhausted even before we set out. Some three or four hours later we got down to the harbour and stumbled over the frozen mud to the low tumbledown hovels with sagging roofs which had been taken over for the commissary stores. Now the commissaries of course were all civilians and as dismal a crew as you would ever hope to meet – shifty broken down clerks and arrogant shop boys that no respectable business would employ and all living in warm huts with two good meals a day. All was muddle and confusion. Nobody knew what stores had been landed or what was still on board the ships. Nothing could be moved without a requisition. Food was left to rot and warm clothing was sent back to Constantinople. Some of the stores were even thrown into the harbour with the dead horses.

Well, Captain Dungate was not to be baffled and after a while he found the hut we wanted and there, thrown into a corner, was a bale of blankets, marked with our regimental number.

'I'll take those,' says the Captain to the commissary clerk.

'That you will not,' says the commissary, and prattles on about the requisitions and the regulations and the signatures and all the rest of it.

'For God's sake man!' says the Captain, 'We are digging men out of their graves for their blankets. I must have that bale. I will sign for them myself on a regimental warrant and these men can carry them back to their comrades in the hospital tent.'

But the more he argued the more obstinate the commissary stood against him, and refused to do anything without the proper papers. It made me mad to see that young officer bullied by such a disreputable creature but in the end there was nothing to be done.

'I'm sorry boys,' says the Captain, 'there's no help for it. We must go back and come again later with another requisition.'

You can well imagine with what heavy hearts we climbed back to the camp, and snatched an hour's sleep until night fell and we were told off again into the trenches. There was nothing doing the next day, for we were all too exhausted to make the journey again, but the captain says, 'We'll try again tomorrow' and soon after first light five or six of us set off once more down the road. It was no better than before, and the cold was worse if anything, but every step took us nearer and we got down to the harbour before noon. Well now, I thought, we shall get some blankets at least, and maybe even a small stove, and that will help some of the lads. But I reckoned without the commissary clerk. He was there again, with his little wispy moustache and his arrogant manners, and not a sign of our blankets in the place.

'What's become of them?' says the Captain, full of anger. 'I have brought the requisition, all properly made out and in good order – where are my things?'

'Oh there's nothing for you,' says the commissary. 'They were for the 77th East Middlesex, and they have all been taken.'

'You scoundrel!' cries the Captain 'They had our number on them as plain as could be – 57th West Middlesex.'

I was no scholar, but I had seen that for myself, and no mistake.

'Oh well,' says the clerk 'They have all gone, and that's all there is to it. You should have had the papers when you came before, you know. You must have the proper requisition at the proper time.'

Then he gave a nervous little snigger and I knew something was up. Some other regiment had bribed him, or he had sold our blankets to some thieving Turks or Frenchmen. Whatever the case, he had made something out of it, and we were the losers. Of course I had no proof but young as I was I had seen enough of his sort to know what his game was and it made me sick to my stomach to see him laughing there.

Well you can imagine me and my mates began to kick up a row, and someone said we should take what we needed, never mind what regiment it was named for. Then the commissary said something about the Mutiny Act and that riled the Captain and he said he would see the man in Hell and I saw his hand go to the strap of his revolver. Now I was only a private soldier, and to catch hold of an officer was a flogging offence, but for all that

I took hold of his arm and spoke a quiet word. He glared at me very hard and for a moment I feared the worst but then he turned on his heel and walked out on to the quay.

'It's no good, Stannard,' says he, when I followed him out with the others, 'It's no good!' (with a dreadful oath).

It would have taken us all day to sort out the muddle and corruption, and then we should have been absent from our duty in the trenches, so we gave it up as a bad job and set off once again to the camp. After a bit the captain says to me, in a thick voice, 'Walk on ahead Stannard,' and I did so and never looked behind me, for I knew he was weeping with rage and frustration.

Well, even the worst of winters must come to an end, and by the end of February the snow began to melt, and the days grew a little longer and we looked about us to see how many men we had lost. Too many, Mr Holmes, too many – old soldiers from Dublin and the garrison towns, married men with children and young men like myself, some them enlisted in the spring and carried off before the year was out.

Then they built a railway, and the stores came steaming up from the harbour twice a day, and when the warm weather came we were swaddled up in Afghan coats and woollen comforters and great fur boots, like so many Eskimo. The rest you know, I am sure. We opened up the bombardments again and stormed the Malakoff, and at the finish Sevastopol had fallen and the Russian fleet was destroyed.

We stayed on in the East for a second winter but by now we had huts and stoves and new uniforms and no more pickets in the trenches, so we slept warm and dry at night and watched the officers racing their horses during the day. Captain Dungate made me his orderly, and we sailed home to England in the Autumn of 1856.

Soon afterwards he exchanged into another regiment and purchased promotion, so I saw nothing of him, though I heard from time to time that he was doing well. I served twenty one years with my own regiment. I need not tell you how those years were spent, for a soldier's life is full of incident but I taught myself to read and write and finished up a recruiting sergeant myself, working the same public house in Trafalgar Square, and earning a guinea for every new recruit I brought in. When my time was up in '75 I found work as a gardener in Shoreditch. But a few months later my governor sold up and moved away and I found myself, for the first time in my life, without a situation. Of course I kept my eyes open but times were hard and there was nothing to be had in my line of business so my little savings were soon used up.

Then one day I got hold of the Army List and found out my old officer Captain Dungate. He was now a Lieutenant-Colonel but I knew him to be the same man, so I walked round to Welbeck Street and sent in my name and asked for the favour of a few moments' conversation.

'Why Stannard,' says the Colonel, 'I remember you

very well, and I am sorry to see you down on your luck. Will you show me your discharge?'

So I handed him my parchment certificate, with 'Conduct exemplary' and he was pleased at that, and said it was just what he would have expected.

'Now then,' says he, Have you ever been in private service, waiting at table and so forth?'

Well I had to admit I had not, except of course when I was his camp servant on campaign.

'Never mind,' says he, 'I need a good manservant and the housekeeper can help you along at first. What do you say to eighteen guineas a year all found with a month's warning on either side if we are not suited?'

Well of course I was delighted and accepted at once. I was lucky to have such a good billet and it brings tears to my eyes when I think how I have thrown it all away.

The Colonel and I got on very well, just as we had done in the old days and sometimes, if we had company, he would say, 'This is Stannard, who was with me in the Crimea'. But that aside we did not talk much of the old times. The truth is, we had both seen the horrors of war when we were young men and we did not care to dwell on them as we grew older.

Now I come to the unhappy events which have changed my life so suddenly for the worse.

You know, of course, about the Colonel's dinner party last week. His sister and her husband were regular visitors and their daughter was on very good terms with Miss Violet. The fourth guest, Mr Wilmott, was new to me. I thought he had probably taken a drink or two before he arrived, and there was something about his voice and appearance which made me uneasy.

The meal went well enough, and at the end the ladies retired and I stayed to clear the things away in my basket while the Colonel and the other two gentlemen passed round the port. The Colonel's brother-in-law was always a very quiet gentleman, but Mr Wilmott had been drinking too well, and began to make rather a noise. He was a banker but he boasted that he had done all sorts of jobs in his time, including pawnbroker and commissary clerk. Then of course I pricked up my ears, and a moment later he was talking about his time at Balaclava, and some 'little opportunities' which had come his way.

'Oh yes,' he said, 'There was plenty to be done for a sharp young fellow, especially when the regimental officers were so green!'

And then he gave a nasty little snigger and I knew in an instant who he was, for I remembered his wispy little moustache and his arrogant ways. I looked across at the Colonel and he glanced at me, just for an instant, and we both knew we had found the same man. Wilmott never recognised us of course, and no wonder, for we soldiers had all worn great thick beards on that campaign, officers and men alike, by special permission of the Queen. Indeed I kept mine on all through my time in the Army and only shaved it off when I moved to Shoreditch.

As soon as we exchanged glances in that way the Colonel stood up very briskly and said 'Shall we join the ladies?' and without waiting for an answer strode out of the room.

Then they had their few minutes with the ladies, with the Colonel saying hardly a word. I guessed he was thinking of the old times, and all the men we lost, and all the villains like Wilmott who would not lift a hand to help them. Pretty soon the Colonel said he was feeling poorly and proposed to make an early night of it. I knew of course that he just wanted an excuse to get Wilmott out of the house.

The party broke up, and I went out to call a four wheeler for the Colonel's sister and her family. They offered Wilmott a seat but he said it was a fine night and he only lived only five minutes away and chose to walk home for the exercise. So the cab drove off, and Wilmott set off on foot. The Colonel and Miss Violet stepped back into the house. I waited a moment and as soon as the cab was out of sight I closed the front door behind me and marched down the street after Wilmott. I wanted a word with this man, before he went home to sleep easy in his bed.

I caught up with him at the end of the street and stood squarely in front of him. I told him how he had pained the Colonel with his foolish boasting, and how we remembered him very well from Balaclava. Then he began to curse me for a low ruffian that did not deserve my place, and said I had only waylaid him for his money and he would call a constable, and much more besides.

He was carrying a black stick with a big silver knob,

and he started to wave this about in his excitement. Well the more heated he was, the more angry and indignant I became, for I thought, What right has he to threaten me in this way! Then suddenly he struck out at me with his infernal stick. Now a little commissary clerk in drink was no match for an old recruiting sergeant and in an instant I had wrested the stick from his grasp and struck him across the arm. Then, God forgive me, I struck a second blow, with all my might. This time it landed on his temple. He dropped like a stone, and never stirred a muscle.

I stood there for a moment, quite helpless, then flung the stick away and took to my heels. I ducked into the mews, ran down to the end, and scrambled over the back garden wall. Two minutes later I was back in the house. I was panting like a dog, and hoping against hope that no-one had seen me. As luck would have it the maid had left some time before and Mrs Finch was still down in the kitchen. I had no wound and not a speck of blood on me, that I could see. So I sat quiet and thought, perhaps I might yet be safe.

I thought I had killed the man outright and I had no remorse. He had lived and died a bully and he had got nothing but his just deserts. But I had no wish to swing for him and I knew as I stood in the back hall, what a d——d fool I had been, and how soon the police would be on to me. I resolved to speak to the Colonel without a moment's delay. However that was easier said than done, for he was still in the drawing room, and speaking to

Miss Violet. Of course he knew nothing of what had happened in the street but I knew Wilmott's boasting had upset him and I supposed he was taking a few minutes to calm his nerves and recover his composure. When we have seen something ugly we like to turn our mind to what is quiet and beautiful.

I don't know what they talked about – nothing in particular I now believe – and I was half mad with fear, but I had to bide my time. Mrs Finch soon finished her work and said goodnight, but it was over an hour before Miss Violet went up to her room and I found the Colonel alone. Then I told him everything, just as I have set it down here. He sat very quiet and his face was stone, and when I had finished, 'Why have you told me this, John?' he says, using my first name. 'I dare say there was not another living soul knew what you had done and now I know everything and you have put me in a false position.'

Well, I had not looked at it in that light, and now I was sorry again, but what was said could not be taken back, so I just stood there in a daze, and supposed I should be taken into custody. But the Colonel soon spoke up again.

'Well, John,' he said, 'I shall shed no tears for Wilmott, and there was a time when I might have finished him myself. I am not going to perjure myself at my time of life, nor make a fool of myself on your account, but I will put myself out of the way for a little while. If I am not here the authorities cannot ask me any questions and I can't give them any answers. But you must stay put and keep silent. If you run they will suspect you at once and you will be taken up. Time enough to go when the dust has settled, and then I can return.'

With that he gave me a year's wages, less a guinea, which he said was all the cash he had in the house, and packed his valise. I thanked him as best I could and he left. That was the last I ever saw of him, or ever expected to see. I never knew he had left a note for Miss Violet or taken her emerald, and I do not know now why he did so.

The rest you know. Wilmott was not dead as I thought, but he died pretty soon after. The police found his pocket book and came round to Welbeck Street the following morning. I knew now what I had to do. I just gave my account of the dinner party, and said nothing about recognising the man. At the finish I said I had called the cab, and seen the guests off, and then stepped back into the house and locked up. That was all in the regular way and I left them to think that Wilmott must have been surprised by some robber in the street. Of course I made it plain that the Colonel had no hand in it. As to his going away, I made light of that and said he would be back again directly. I could not tell Miss Violet what had happened, or even hint at it, but I did my best to reassure her that in due time all would be well.

Then as you know, Mr Holmes, she consulted you about the case and I had to face your questions when you called at the house. I did my best to keep steady and calm but something in your manner made me think you knew more than you cared to say. The following day I saw the Colonel's advertisement in the *Morning Post*. I did not know what had decided him to come back so soon, but I was still a free man and the same evening I walked out of Welbeck Street and into exile.

Thank God, I have no wife or daughter of my own to share my disgrace. Whether you meant to help me on my way I shall never know but if you did I am very glad of it for it is better than I deserve.

> Yours truly,
> John Stannard

'Does Miss Dungate know of this?' I asked, putting down the letter.

'Not if her father has kept his own counsel,' said Holmes, 'which I fancy he may have done. Old men have their secrets, which they carry to the grave.'

'Did you suspect the man?'

'I was certain of his guilt when I saw that some fit and active person had recently scaled the wall into the garden and had left no evidence of departing by the same route. I assumed that this resourceful individual was neither the maid nor the housekeeper. That left only Stannard, and respectable manservants do not resort to such expedients except in a case of sudden emergency. Nor is an old soldier reticent about the name of his regiment unless he hopes to discourage further questions. Of course I could not guess the cause of Wilmott's quarrel, nor how far the Colonel was implicated, but the reference to blankets suggested some military, or possibly medical, connection. Whatever the cause, this was clearly a sudden disagreement, for the assassin had no weapon of his own and the fatal blow had been struck with the victim's own stick.'

'Why did you not confide in Hopkins?'

'Really Watson,' said Holmes, in an exasperated tone, 'I cannot be responsible for the deficiencies of Scotland Yard in every case I undertake. My obligation was to Miss Dungate and her father. Let that suffice.'

'As to Miss Dungate,' I asked, 'why did her father take her emerald?'

'That I am sure was no more than a temporary measure. He had parted with his ready cash to Stannard and was resolved to stay away for some time. It might not have been prudent to correspond with his bankers and although he would never have parted with the emerald it might have stood pledge for a cash advance had the need arisen.'

We stood together at the window, looking down at the straw hats and parasols in the bustling street below. As we did so our thoughts returned to Stannard's letter, and the terrible winter of 1854.

'It was a bad business, Watson,' said Holmes 'and carried off so many fine young men. Let us be thankful for the warmth of an English summer and the great legacy of the *Pax Britannica*.'

THE WOODBRIDGE SOLICITOR

SOME of the heavier cases in which my friend Sherlock Holmes was engaged absorbed the whole of his attention for weeks on end, depriving him of sleep and draining his energy, at some risk even to his remarkable constitution. At other times the pace was slower, and he was able to break off from a long case for a day or two, to attend to some other intriguing mystery which had caught his fancy.

So it was in the autumn of 1895, when the barometer had begun to fall, there was a chill in the air and the leaves were scurrying across the pavements. Not ten days had passed since the horrible discoveries at the Maison des Effardes in the Rue St Lazare. Holmes had been summoned to the French Embassy and had begun his investigations under conditions of great secrecy. He soon concluded, however, that no further progress could be made until Henderson the deaf mute was discharged from the Charing Cross Hospital and in the meantime he busied himself with his chemical experiments.

In the middle of one such experiment which, being conducted within a few feet of the breakfast table, did little to enhance my appetite, Mrs Hudson brought up a letter. Holmes opened the envelope, glanced at the contents, and tossed the letter and envelope over to me.

'Now Watson, here is a little light relief from the

horrors of the *haute bourgeoisie*!' he said. 'What do you make of it?'

It was a typewritten letter from a firm of solicitors, Hubblecroft & Nephew, of Woodbridge in Suffolk and read as follows—

> *Dear Mr Holmes,*
>
> *Your name has been mentioned to me by Inspector Foulcher, who tells me you were of great assistance to him in the Southwold botanical scandal. May I call at 2.15 tomorrow afternoon? If not please telegraph.*
>
> *Yours sincerely,*
>
> *Wilfred Bellamy*
>
> *PS. My visit is prompted by a most disturbing occurrence at this office on Sunday.*

'And what, I wonder' I said, 'was the disturbing occurrence?'

'I have no idea Watson, and it is idle to speculate. No doubt the police are baffled. Foulcher is methodical enough but entirely without imagination. In the Southwold case he overlooked the significance of a small detail which enabled me to clear up the entire mystery without leaving this room. There may be something of the sort in the present instance.'

'Another botanical scandal perhaps? The Southwold affair does not seem to have been very serious.'

'On the contrary, the happiness of three women was blighted and an honest man was sent to an early grave. But let us return to Mr Bellamy. What do you make of his letter?'

'This is an engraved letterhead of a slightly old fashioned appearance, from a market town in Suffolk. This
suggests a prosperous firm, which has been established
for many years. It names Mr Wilfred Bellamy as the only
partner; no doubt he is the nephew, who inherited the
practice on his uncle Hubblecroft's retirement. He asks
for an afternoon appointment, which suggests a rather
leisurely timetable, and he may be staying the night at his
London club. I expect he is a prosperous middle-aged
legal gentleman and something of an expert on agricultural holdings.'

'Capital Watson! You surpass yourself.'

'One more thing; the letterhead uses the phrase
Attorney and solicitor although common law attorneys were
abolished, I believe, some twenty years ago. This rein-
forces the impression of a conservative firm, which still
favours the old professional title.'

Here I paused, detecting a certain gleam in my friend's
eye, and asked him, 'Do you agree with my conclusions?'

'I cannot concur,' he replied. 'My observations tell me
that Mr Bellamy is an energetic and go-ahead young man,
with some very modern ideas, who has only recently
purchased the Hubblecroft practice after spending some
time in France. He probably knows more of the Code
Napoleon than of agricultural holdings. He acquired the
practice for a modest premium but it has absorbed all his
capital and for the moment he has not a penny to spare.
The outgoing partner who sold him the practice, and
who may indeed have been Hubblecroft's nephew, was

an elderly practitioner who at one time had been very prosperous but whose practice had fallen away in recent years.'

'My dear Holmes!' I cried, 'You know these people already.'

'I assure you I had no idea of their existence until I opened the letter two minutes ago. However the evidence on which I base my conclusions is plain enough. Observe first, that the letter and the envelope are of very different quality. The envelope is well made, in a heavy laid paper, and was supplied by one of the better law stationers. It has however been in store for some years and is beginning to discolour at the edges. The letterhead, by contrast, is printed on a light wove paper, perfectly fresh, with a commercial watermark which I do not recognise. Paper of this sort will soon deteriorate and could only have been chosen for reasons of economy. Thus the paper and the envelope were purchased at different times and for different reasons. The man who laid in a stock of expensive envelopes some years ago had a prosperous practice, and did not expect that as his work declined his stationery would grow yellow with age. Our correspondent uses the old envelopes, but was obliged to order new letterheads to show the change of ownership. He could not afford stationery of the same quality as his predecessor, just as his predecessor could ask no more than a modest premium for a practice which was steadily declining.'

'Well of course,' I said, 'Now that you explain it in that way it is all perfectly simple.'

'Just so,' said Holmes, dryly. 'The letterhead itself has been printed from an engraved die cut in Baskerville old face. The die is well-worn and has been in use for many years, but has recently been modified. A small alteration is presumably cheaper than a new die. Thus the name of the outgoing partner has been blanked out, and Mr Bellamy's name added in a slightly different typeface.'

'What of the go-ahead ideas and the time spent in France?'

'The letter is written on one of the new portable machines, an Oliver possibly or a Blickensderfer, which must have cost him twelve guineas at least. Yet he is reluctant to pay half a crown for a new ribbon as the one he has used is very heavily worn. This shows that he is a man of modern ideas but somewhat limited means. As to the time in France, I direct your attention to a significant correction in the salutation. He began to type 'Dear M. Holmes', in the French style, but having placed the stop after the 'M' instantly realised his mistake, went back, and inserted an 'R'. Only a man habituated to French correspondence would make such an error.'

'That leaves only the question of his youth and the leisurely timetable.'

'The signature is that of a young man, boldly written with a steel pen, and his timetable is not in the least leisurely. On the contrary, he asks for an appointment at an hour which will allow him to attend to his post before he leaves Suffolk in the morning and return in time to despatch his outgoing letters in the evening. I shall see him, of course, since he seems to think his problem warrants a journey to London but whether the case will afford the slightest interest remains to be seen. Why don't you stay and meet him this afternoon my dear fellow, if you have nothing better to do?'

I readily agreed, since I knew from experience that the most unpromising of my friend's cases could sometimes develop in remarkable ways. Nor was I to be disappointed on this occasion.

Our visitor arrived promptly at the appointed time. Mr Wilfred Bellamy was a dapper little man in his middle twenties. Fair in complexion, he had keen darting eyes and a neatly trimmed moustache. His hands were as slender as a woman's and his feet were remarkably small. He spoke fluently and his voice was precise and melodious.

'Please sit down Mr Bellamy,' said Holmes. 'This is my friend and colleague Dr Watson. Pray how can we help you?'

'I do hope gentlemen,' he began, 'that I am not wasting your time with my little problem, but it has given me some anxiety and it is deeply puzzling.'

'Your letter mentioned a disturbing occurrence.' said Holmes, placing his long fingertips together. 'The facts, if you please?'

'First, Mr Holmes, let me tell you something about myself. I was born in Suffolk but have spent most of my life in London. My father died when I was young and my mother has struggled to support us both and pay for my professional education. She has high hopes for me and of course I wish to succeed on her account as well as my own.

'I served my articles with Dixon Weld & Co of Lower James Street. They are a well-established firm with a good reputation and they act as London agents for a number of country solicitors. I was admitted to the roll of solicitors two years ago. I then continued with the firm as a managing clerk. I should add that Dixon Weld & Co also have a small office in Paris, which is where I have been working since January of last year.

'Some weeks ago, on one of my visits to the London office, I heard that one of our "country solicitors" as we call them was soon to retire. He was Mr Hubblecroft of Woodbridge, who at one time had sent us a great deal of work. He was now in his seventies and since he had no son or junior partner was obliged to sell up. I went to see him and found he had a family practice which he had inherited from his uncle. Twenty years ago it had been very prosperous but in recent years the work had fallen away. Between ourselves, gentlemen, I believe that Mr Hubblecroft's advancing years had made him somewhat slow and although a very methodical man he was somewhat set in his ways. It seemed to me that a younger man, with more energy and some new ideas of his own, would be able to work the practice up again. As there was no other buyer in the offing I made him an offer to purchase the business for £100 down and the balance by instalments over the next five years, which he was pleased to accept.

'As it happened my tour of duty in the Paris office was coming to an end and my employers were good enough to release me on short notice, so I moved down to Woodbridge, took a room at the Bull and took over the business at Michaelmas quarter day, three weeks ago. I have had a very busy time of it, as you can imagine. Mr Hubblecroft remained in the office for the first two weeks, introducing me to his clients and some of the other professional gentlemen in Woodbridge, but he has now departed and I have to make my own way. So you see gentlemen, this regrettable incident has come at a most unfortunate time, just when I need to establish myself as a steady and reliable newcomer to the town.'

'The facts!' said Holmes, in his rather abrupt way.

'Today is Wednesday. Some time on Sunday my office on Market Hill was broken into. A door at the rear of the premises was prised open with some implement. It was a neat job and Inspector Foulcher, whom of course I consulted, believes it may have been the work of a professional burglar.'

Holmes gave a slight sigh and a look of impatience crossed his face at the thought that this was, after all, nothing more than a commonplace provincial burglary.

'Do you have a list of the property stolen?' he asked.

'Nothing was stolen Mr Holmes.' Here our visitor paused and produced a small packet from his waistcoat pocket. 'On the contrary, my burglar left me a present of ten guineas, that is to say ten and a half sovereigns,' saying which he opened the packet and showed us the coins. Holmes leaned forward to inspect them, and as he did so it seemed to me that his features sharpened and his manner became more attentive.

'Where were these found?' he asked.

'Neatly stacked on my desk, Mr Holmes, which is in the front room on the first floor of the building, overlooking the Market Square. I found them on Monday morning when I opened up the office and discovered the break in, and beneath the coins was this note.' saying which he handed Holmes a sheet of blue foolscap paper on which, in block capitals, was typed the following—

REGRET MANTELPIECE MR LIFE & DEATH

'The paper is my own, and the message had clearly been typed on my own machine, which stands on a small table to the side of my desk. As soon as I read it I examined the mantelpiece and found that it had indeed been slightly damaged. It is a wooden mantelpiece, grained and varnished, on which I keep a carriage clock and one or two other items. Some of these things had been moved to clear a space at one end and in that space a straight line had been heavily scored. It was at an angle, across the whole width of the mantelpiece. The man had evidently used my steel ruler and a bodkin which I use for sewing up documents, both of which were near at hand. I noticed that the tip of the bodkin bore some traces of varnish. The damage can be made good but I do not take kindly to such an act of vandalism.'

'Hardly vandalism,' said Holmes, 'for your intruder took no pleasure in damaging your property.'

'It seems to me,' I said, 'the act of a madman.'

'Man or woman, there is motive here, not madness,'

said Holmes as he studied the typewritten message, 'but the motive is certainly obscure.'

'Inspector Foulcher was as puzzled as myself and had never come across anything of the sort before. It was then that he recommended I should come to you, as he thought the case might be rather more in your line than his.'

'It certainly presents one or two unusual features,' said Holmes. 'Have you spoken to anyone else about this note?'

'No, for I do not wish to encourage speculation and gossip.'

'Do you employ any clerks?'

'Just one, a smart young fellow who was recommended by Mr Hubblecroft and is hoping to study the law himself. But he is from a very respectable family, and of course has the run of the office every day. He is looking after it today, in my absence, and has no reason to force an entry, still less to leave me a present of ten guineas.'

'Have you had any unusual visitors since you took over the practice?'

'No one out of the ordinary, and all Mr Hubblecroft's clients are most respectable.'

'Then he had no criminal practice?'

'Oh no, he was not a criminal lawyer and would have been quite at a loss in that type of work, as indeed I am myself. Anything of that sort is generally referred to Amwells, in Cumberland Street.'

'Do I take it you have now moved out of the Bull and are sleeping in your business premises?'

'Not yet,' said Bellamy, evidently somewhat embarrassed by my friend's question, 'but as you have guessed I propose to do so. In point of fact I have fitted out a small bedroom next to my office. The furniture was delivered last week and I shall move in this evening or tomorrow. It will be a saving of expense, you understand, and I shall also be on hand to deal with any further intrusion.'

'Have you asked Mr Hubblecroft if he can throw any light on the matter?' I asked.

'I cannot do so, Dr Watson,' Mr Bellamy replied. 'As I mentioned he spent a fortnight introducing me to the practice but he has now left for a short holiday and I believe is fishing on the Hampshire Avon. I do not expect him to return to Suffolk for another three or four weeks.'

'It is fortunate', said Holmes, 'that I have a day or two at my disposal, and as your case is not without interest I shall be happy to look into it. May I suggest that Dr Watson and myself catch the early train tomorrow morning and present ourselves at your offices at ten-fifteen?'

'That would be most kind,' said Bellamy, but may I ask one more thing before we part? The note refers to a matter of life and death. Do you suppose that could be true?'

'I cannot imagine that your mysterious intruder would have taken the trouble to say so were it not the case.'

With that our visitor departed. Holmes strode over to his bookshelf and took down a well-worn copy of Archbold's Criminal Pleading and Practice which he studied for a few minutes. Then, replacing the volume with a smile of satisfaction and making a note in his pocket book, he returned to his chemical apparatus.

* * *

The following morning found us seated in a first class railway carriage and absorbed in our newspapers as the line, at first overshadowed by the drab furniture workshops of Shoreditch, soon carried us over the busy streets and tramways of East London and out into the open fields and small farmlands of Essex. After a while Holmes tossed aside his paper and took from his pocket the small packet of sovereigns which our client had left with us.

'Is there anything to be learned from the coins?' I asked.

'The coins themselves tell us nothing,' said Holmes, 'but the amount may be significant. The English are peculiar in their reckoning of money. The tradesman deals in pounds, shillings and pence, the milliner's creations are priced in shillings and professional men such as yourself deal only in guineas, though the last guinea coin was struck in the reign of George III.'

'Why do you suppose the burglar left the money?'

'Because he was sorry for what he had done, and wished to make amends.'

'Any yet he had taken nothing.'

'On the contrary, I have no doubt he took something of the first importance. It may have been a document, or merely some confidential information but his courteous note suggests that he has no intention of returning, from which I infer that he found what he was looking for.'

'Yet Bellamy says he missed nothing.'

'Bellamy has bought an old family practice. Hubble-croft and his uncle before him have been accumulating papers for fifty years or more. There must be thousands of documents gathering dust in cupboards and deed boxes. How could he know if any one document was missing? As Confucius observes, it is not easy to find a black cat in a dark room – especially if there is no cat.'

'Then there is the damage to the mantelpiece, which must surely be the most puzzling feature of the case.'

'Now there Watson I cannot agree with you. The solution to that particular problem is elementary, though not without a certain significance.'

I knew from experience that there was no hope of any further explanation when my friend was in this humour and returned to my newspaper as the train sped on towards Suffolk.

An hour or so later our train pulled into the quayside by the River Deben and we had arrived in Woodbridge. We walked briskly up the hill to the main thoroughfare and turned into the police station where Inspector Foulcher was waiting to meet us. He was a handsome, clean-shaven man with a warm handshake and the gentle lilting speech of the Suffolk coast.

'It is good of you to come down here gentlemen,' he said 'but then I believe this case is in your line of country, Mr Holmes. It is a peculiar business and not like anything I have seen before. Now if you come along with me we shall step up and see young Mr Bellamy.'

So saying he led the way as we walked to the main square in the upper part of the town. It was not a market day and apart from a young girl minding a pony and trap the square was quiet. Its sleepy houses and a few shops overlooked the shire hall, a lofty elegant building in the Dutch style which stood alone in the centre of the square. A few more paces brought us to a small building on the north side, whose gleaming brass plate identified the offices of Hubblecroft and Nephew. Mr Bellamy was evidently expecting us and came downstairs just as we arrived.

'Before we look over your rooms, Mr Bellamy' said Inspector Foulcher, 'I should like to show Mr Holmes and Dr Watson where your burglar got in.'

'Of course,' said Bellamy, 'Let me take you round the side of the building.'

We followed him out of the front door and turned into a narrow passageway which led to a small yard at the rear. I could see then that behind the neat brick frontages facing on to the square many of the houses were old timber-framed buildings, which had been standing here since Tudor times. Mr Bellamy's property was no exception and appeared to have been somewhat neglected in recent years.

'This is the door that was forced, Mr Holmes,' said the Inspector. He indicated a plain wooden door in the side of what had once been a wash house or scullery which jutted out from the rear of the building.

'As you see,' said Bellamy, 'a new lock has been fitted

since the intrusion but otherwise this is just as I found it.'

'And here,' said Foulcher, 'is where the old lock was forced. Now you know how it is, Mr Holmes, with our young housebreakers. They like to carry a small crowbar or jemmy as they call it which gives them a swagger and is ready to hand as a useful weapon if they are surprised. But this door has not been forced with a crowbar, for the bruise on the frame, as you see, is four inches wide. Our man has used a bolster or cold chisel which is made to lift floorboards. It will force a door as well as any crowbar and yet it fits snug into a man's pocket. It is what the old hands use, Mr Holmes, and they call it a persuader.'

Holmes nodded in agreement and Foulcher continued.

'Even so, it was not an easy job, for this is a good strong door, and he had to set about it quiet and slow. And here,' he said, reaching into his pocket and producing a small piece of wood, 'is another clue. I found this just inside the door. It is an old dodge: a wedge to close the door from the inside when the lock has been forced. That way there is nothing to alert suspicion if anyone should happen by. So I'd say our housebreaker was an old lag. I'll wager he wears elastic-sided boots which he can slip off to go on tip-toe in his stockinged feet and most likely he carries a lump of coal in his pocket for good luck.'

Holmes nodded, again seemingly lost in thought, then suddenly asked, 'What room is that?'

I followed his glance as he looked up to a window on the first floor. This was a large casement, almost directly above the low roof of the old wash house.

'That is the window to what Mr Hubblecroft called his cabinet room,' said Bellamy 'which I will show you directly. It had been shut fast for many years but the room was so musty I threw open the casement as soon as I arrived. Now I find the frame is warped and will not shut properly. I meant to engage a carpenter to put it right, but with so many other things to attend to I have quite overlooked it.'

'Your visitor would not have done so' said Holmes, 'for it would have saved him some trouble. Watson, do you suppose you could get on to the roof and in through the window?'

'I will do it now, if you wish.' I said. 'I can climb on to the coal bunker, clamber on to the wash house roof and be inside in less than half a minute. Nor should I be spotted, for we are not overlooked. The next house on this side is built further back, and that on the other appears to be vacant.'

'Good old Watson!' cried Holmes. 'You have missed your profession, my friend, and with a lump of coal in your pocket will yet make a capital housebreaker. But we shall not put you to the test just now. Mr Bellamy, will you take us in and show us your room?'

The four of us entered through the rear door and went upstairs. Bellamy's room was at the front of the building, overlooking the square. It was plainly furnished and somewhat shabby but remarkably neat and tidy. On his desk, which stood in front of the sash windows, his clients' papers were carefully arranged while waiting his attention, each file neatly bundled and tied up with pink tape.

Holmes strode across to the mantelpiece on which was the singular mark, deeply scored in the surface of the wood, exactly as it had been described to us. He took out his glass and began to examine the mark together with the ruler and the bodkin alongside it.

'You can see how our man could have set to work undisturbed,' said Foulcher. There are lace curtains on the lower sashes of these windows. No-one passing below can look up into this room and the shire hall blocks the view from the other side of the square.'

'The curtains were Mr Hubblecroft's idea,' Bellamy explained. 'He was most particular about keeping his client's affairs private, and some clients, he believed, would not wish to be seen in consultation with him.'

'Indeed,' said Holmes, taking out his pocket watch. 'Have the goodness to step away from the window will you?'

Bellamy did so, though clearly puzzled by this request, and my friend gave a little cry of satisfaction. 'Just as I thought!' he said. 'See how, in this bright sunlight, the shadow of the sash window falls across the mantelpiece. It aligns, very nearly, with the mark your intruder made. This is an improvised sundial. He was here shortly before eleven o'clock in the morning and wished to make a permanent record of that fact.'

'But why should he do such a thing?' asked Bellamy.

'To lay the ground for a false alibi, perhaps?' I suggested.

'Hardly so, for that would suggest a carefully laid plan

while the use of Mr Bellamy's ruler and bodkin suggest something done on the spur of the moment. And here is something else. Look here, Inspector, using my lens: a tiny mark in the wallpaper at the back of the mantelpiece. Now, if I place the steel ruler here, just as our man must have done when he scored the line, we can see how this second mark exactly corresponds to the width of the ruler.'

'Oh you are right there sure enough,' said Inspector Foulcher, 'but the second mark is so small, I had quite overlooked it.'

'That is because you were not expecting to find it,' said Holmes. 'I looked for it because in my view it has particular significance.'

'Well I don't know about that,' said Inspector Foulcher, 'for I can't see it adds much to the case.'

'That remains to be seen,' said Holmes. 'And this is your typewriter?' he asked, turning to Bellamy.

'A gift from my mother when I passed my final examinations.' Holmes paused in front of the Oliver, and with his long index finger gently turned the ribbon spool.

'Now be kind enough to show us your cabinet room.'

'It is through here,' said Bellamy, opening a door just behind us. We stepped in and I could see at once that the room was aptly named, for the walls were lined from floor to ceiling with a fine set of mahogany cabinets. Each cabinet was about eighteen inches square and furnished with its own brass catch and a flap which opened downwards. Some of these flaps had paper labels bearing the names of individual clients, such as *Billing's and Osborne's Charity* and *Lippincott's will trusts.* Many were simply labelled with a single letter of the alphabet, neatly penned in a black letter script. There was no other furniture, apart from a small ladder and a single gas bracket in the ceiling. The atmosphere was still somewhat musty, with the distinctive smell of old vellum and parchment, and I could understand why Bellamy had thrown open the window which we had seen from the yard below.

'I must tell you gentlemen,' said Bellamy, 'that Mr Hubblecroft took a special pride in this room. All his old papers were filed away here, in alphabetical order, and each in the proper cabinet. They must go back forty or fifty years and his boast was that he could always put his hand on anything he wanted.'

We looked into one or two of the cabinets, where the bundles of papers were stacked one on top of the other.

'Why these are like little Egyptian mummies!' said Inspector Foulcher, with a laugh, 'all buried away in this sarcophagus – as if they should still be here a hundred years from now.'

'Yet I think one or two may have seen the light of day already,' murmured Holmes, as we returned through Bellamy's office and stepped across the landing to the adjoining room. Here were his bachelor sleeping quarters which, with one or two prints and a few ornaments, he had contrived to make a little more cheerful than his office.

'There is nothing more to show you here, gentlemen,' he said. 'On the ground floor is only the front office, where my young clerk sits, and a waiting room at the rear.

'What can you tell me about the other solicitors in Woodbridge?' asked Holmes.

'I have yet to meet them all,' Bellamy replied, 'There are no more than half a dozen here in Woodbridge and in our neighbouring town of Wickham Market. One or two have already paid me a courtesy visit and I hope to meet some others this evening. The local professional men, that is the doctors and solicitors, have a small supper club which meets once a quarter and I have been invited to attend. I was also encouraged to bring a guest but I fear that will not be possible as I have yet to make any friends in these parts.'

'Why you must take Dr Watson!' cried Holmes, 'This is very much in his line, for he has made a particular study of medico-legal matters and will be excellent company for the evening.'

'I hesitate to ask you on such a slight acquaintance, Dr Watson, but you would of course be most welcome to come as my guest.'

'I am honoured by the invitation,' I replied 'though I hasten to add that my interest in medico-legal matters is only that of an amateur and as a chronicler of my friend's adventures.'

'In the meantime,' asked Inspector Foulcher, 'will you continue your enquiries, Mr Holmes?'

'I must return to London this afternoon,' said Holmes, 'but I will communicate with Dr Watson in the morning. Until then, may I suggest that Mr Bellamy and yourself should give this matter no further thought. It may indeed be a question of life and death but I am quite satisfied there is no immediate danger.'

We parted from Bellamy and walked back to the police station where we left Inspector Foulcher. As soon as the two of us were alone Holmes said 'Well done, Watson! You took the hint and your presence at the club tonight will be quite invaluable.'

'What am I to do?'

'Enjoy your supper, whilst paying close attention to the solicitors. Have the goodness to compile a list of their names as soon as the meeting is over, with a note of their ages and appearance, and if possible the nature of their work. You may disregard any able-bodied man under the age of thirty but I particularly wish to know of anyone who is left-handed. If any solicitor does not attend tonight's meeting, discover what you can about him in his absence.'

'You may rely on me, but have you no time to explain further?'

'No, for I must be in Chancery Lane no later than four this afternoon and the train leaves in less than fifteen minutes.'

He quickened his pace towards the railway station, leaving me to find accommodation at the Bull, and then stroll round the town until the time fixed for the supper club that evening. That proved to be a most convivial occasion. We were fifteen in number: six doctors and nine solicitors. Bellamy, I was glad to see, fitted in well with the company, and seemed to be well-received, and one of my fellow practitioners gave me news of young Stamford whom I had known at Bart's. Throughout the evening I took care to follow Holmes's instructions, committing to memory everything I was told about the solicitors and their various fields of practice. When the party broke up, shortly before midnight, I retired to my room and wrote out some notes of what I had learned.

* * *

As I sat in the breakfast room the following morning, sipping coffee and reading the newspaper, I felt a hand on my shoulder and a moment later Holmes was seated at the table and ordering up his own breakfast.

'How did you get on in Chancery Lane?' I asked.

'The Law Society's librarian is most accommodating and I spent an hour or two in the high gallery studying the Law Lists for the last thirty years. And now we shall compare notes. You have your list and I have mine. Pray begin with yours and tell me first if any member of the company was left-handed?'

'That I can answer, for I paid close attention while we were at table. The only left-handed solicitor is George Amwell.'

'What can you tell me about him?'

'He is a large, amiable man in his sixties, somewhat overweight but otherwise in good health. I am told he is generally a very jovial fellow although last night he appeared a little quiet and withdrawn. His practice is in Castle Street and he is mainly a property lawyer, but I believe some firms also send him any criminal work which comes their way.'

'Capital!' said Holmes, consulting his own list. 'George Amwell was admitted to the roll of solicitors in 1852. He has practised in Woodbridge for many years, and is a commissioner for oaths. From 1868 to 1891 he was also Clerk of the Peace to the Borough Quarter Sessions at Ipswich. Are you sure there were no other left-handed men?'

'None, and I think there were no absentees, for the supper club appeared to have a full attendance.'

'Then you may strike through the rest of your list and as soon as we have finished this excellent breakfast we shall walk across the square and acquaint Mr Bellamy with the results of our investigations.'

'Holmes,' I said, for I could see clearly where this was leading, 'it is obvious that you suspect Amwell, though you have yet to tell me your reasons, but have you considered how grave will be the consequences if you should be mistaken in this matter? A false accusation would be horrible. May I tell you my own thoughts about the case?'

'I should be most interested to hear them.'

'The intruder is a man who can use a typewriter but still resorts to abbreviation. He writes "mr" for "matter". He has perhaps been seeking out some scandalous or compromising information with a view to publication or exposure. Does this not point to some disreputable Grub Street journalist, a man who may have no connection with Woodbridge, but may know more about Mr Hubblecroft's clients than we have yet learned? Would it not be wise to delay, at least until Hubblecroft returns from his fishing holiday in Hampshire?'

'No, Watson, a penny-a-line scribbler does not distribute largesse in guineas. But you may put your mind at rest, for I shall say nothing until our quarry has been flushed out and has condemned himself out of his own mouth. Come now, the game's afoot!'

With that we left the hotel and walked across the square to Bellamy's office.

'Good morning gentlemen,' he said eagerly. 'Have you any news for me.'

'I expect to name the intruder within the hour,' said Holmes, 'but first I must ask you to consider whether that is what you truly wish. Before you answer, pray remember that this curious episode is unlikely to be repeated, that neither you nor your practice has come to any serious harm, and that the truth, when it emerges, may be deeply embarrassing for your position in this town.'

'If you can discover the man,' said Bellamy, 'I beg you to do so, for I should never rest content if I thought the truth had been withheld from me.'

'Very well,' said Holmes, 'then if you have an hour to spare I suggest you take up your hat and accompany Dr Watson and myself. For the moment at least I do not think we shall trouble Inspector Foulcher.'

Mr Amwell's office was but a few minutes walk away, in a small, single fronted Georgian house at the upper end of Cumberland Street. Its only advertisement was a small brass plate by the front door, half polished away over the years and bearing the simple legend 'Amwell solicitor'. The three of us stepped in through the front door and found ourselves in a front room where a elderly clerk sat at a high desk, behind a counter.

'We should like to see Mr Amwell, if you please,' said Holmes.

'Are you expected, gentlemen?' asked the clerk.

'No,' said Holmes, 'but I think if you give Mr Amwell this he will be disposed to see us right away,' saying which he handed over his card on the back of which he had written:

24 & 25 Vict cap 96, s. 1

The clerk disappeared for a full three minutes, and then emerged without a word to show us into the inner office. As he left I noticed he took pains to close the door through which we had entered and an internal, baize-covered door, for added privacy. We found ourselves in a dark, old-fashioned room, the single window looking onto a courtyard at the rear. In contrast to Mr Bellamy's room which, although shabby, was neat and trim, Mr Amwell's untidy office reminded me of our comfortable old rooms in Baker Street. Books, papers, files, survey-ors' drawings, briefs to counsel, and abstracts of title were piled up and scattered everywhere, some loose, some in black tin boxes, and some bulging out of brown paper packets. Here and there a discarded length of pink tape snaked across the carpet and once again I noticed that distinctive smell of old parchment deeds. A large clock on the mantelpiece broke the silence with a heavy tick and the outside world seemed to have been banished for ever behind the baize door.

Seated at the table, with his back to the window, was George Amwell. I was shocked at his appearance. No longer the large, amiable man I had met the night before, he seemed to have crumpled in his seat and his face looked grey and sad. Holmes's card was on the desk in front of him.

'Come in gentlemen,' he said, wearily. 'Come in Bellamy, Dr Watson and you, Sir, who must be Mr Sherlock Holmes.' Then he added, glancing down at the card, 'I see you have found me out.'

'So it was you, Mr Amwell,' said Wilfred Bellamy. 'I can hardly believe it, Sir. I think you owe me an explanation.'

'My dear Bellamy,' said Amwell, 'Believe me, I am truly sorry for what has happened. You shall have your explanation, for I have done no more than I believed was right and just. All I ask now gentlemen, is that you take a seat and hear me out and then judge for yourselves whether I have acted for the best.'

We sat down in a semi-circle, facing his desk, Sherlock Holmes with his head slumped forward on his chin, but attentive to every word. After pausing to collect his thoughts Mr Amwell began.

'A little more than three weeks ago I was consulted by a gentleman I had never met before. His name was Captain McKinlock and he called in unexpectedly on a Monday morning. He was a prosperous-looking man of about my own age, an old seafarer, with a wrinkled brown face, a straggling beard, and a very direct way of talking.

"Now sir," said he, "before this interview gets under way I need to know that it will all be close and secret. Nothing must go beyond this room."

"Why of course," I replied, "that goes without saying."

"But I want you to say it, and to shake hands on it."

"I assure you there is no need for this, Captain McKinlock, but since you ask, here is my hand on it, and you have my assurance."

"Well now that's settled, I will tell you my case. I am the registered owner of the brig *Sunrise*, which works the German ocean, on a regular run between Hamburg and Ipswich. She's a good ship of 280 tons and makes a good profit. And now I see by your face you may have heard of her?"

"Is that the vessel from which the first officer went missing, and two members of the crew have been arrested? It was in the papers some weeks ago."

"The very same: Wade and Baldomero are the men. They were taken at Ipswich and sent for trial at the Assizes on a charge of murder. I know nothing of the details, but it seems there was some private quarrel before they left Hamburg and the two men took their revenge on the High Seas.

"Now I must go back a bit," said the Captain, "and tell you of my childhood sweetheart, Verity Müller – Verity Anders as she was then. I knew her forty years ago when her father had a ships' chandler's store here in Woodbridge, and she was a pretty little thing. I set my cap at her, and so did my friend Davy Müller. He was a German boy, very smart in his appearance, and the finish of it was, she chose him instead of me and he carried her off to Hamburg to be married.

"However, all's fair in love and war, and after a bit there were no hard feelings. She and Davy came over here every so often to see her people and then, like as not, the three of us would meet up and sink a glass to the old days.

"Davy had a middling head for business, and he got to buy one or two little boats and lived fairly comfortable. But his chest was bad, and getting worse and in the end he just faded away and died, leaving everything to Verity. Now she was twice as smart as him. Left on her own she worked the business up in a spanking good way, so before long the widow Müller was better known in Hamburg than her husband had ever been.

"Now I come to the secret part of my story. Early in 1870 Verity came over to England and looked me up again.

'Oh Archie,' she says, just as winning as ever, 'Oh Archie, I have a chance to buy a real big ship at last. She's a 100 foot brig, just fitting out in Kiel, and I can run her between here and Hamburg with a master and a crew of six. She's called the *Sonnenaufgang*, which means *Sunrise* and I can pick her up very cheap, as the firm for which she was a-building has suddenly failed. However, I can't afford the whole outlay myself, and I need a partner to come in with me. So why don't we go halves on the ship Archie? Half on the investment and half on the profits? I can look after her in Hamburg and you can look after her in Ipswich. There's plenty of trade that way, and we'll never be short of a cargo.'

"Then she showed me the architect's drawings, and told me something of the yard where she was building, so I was soon persuaded, and agreed to put up half the money, just as she asked. Then of course we had to register the vessel."

'Now Archie,' says she, 'You know there is going to be a war!'

'Oh is there Verity?' said I, smiling at her funny ways.

"Of course there is, Archie. There's trouble brewing between the French and the Prussians and before the year is out they'll be at it hammer and tongs. Now you know what that means; they will both be out in the German ocean, seizing each other's ships and cargoes and all us honest folk will be the losers.'

'Why what's this to us Verity? Our ship will fly the red ensign and that can never be seized, for you know Britannia rules the waves!'

'That's the very point,' says Verity. 'She must be registered at the London Custom House as a British ship, and you must declare that you are a British subject (which you are) and the sole owner, and that no foreigner has any interest in the vessel.'

'Why where's the need for that?' I said. 'You are a British subject and can have your name in the Register along with mine.'

'Now that's where you're wrong,' says Verity, 'for you know I was born in Denmark, and my father was Danish, and I never saw England until I was six weeks old. Then of course Davy was a German, and I have lived in Hamburg all these years so the fact is, I am a foreigner in the eyes of the law.'

"Well all that was news to me, but I thought – what's the harm in it, for Verity was Suffolk bred, as good as the next girl, and I was not the one to disappoint her. She was all in a rush to get the business done, so within a few days I went up to the Custom House and named myself as the sole owner of the brig *Sunrise*. Of course, when I made the declaration the officer gave me the regular warning, which is, should the declaration be false the vessel will be sailing under false colours and forfeit to Her Majesty. However, I thought, that is a risk we shall have to take, and it was too late to go back then, so I held my tongue and trusted all would be well.

"Verity was right enough about the Prussians, of course, and war broke out that very summer, but so long as she flew the red ensign the *Sunrise* was safe enough. She plied back and forth, just as we had planned, and has brought us in a tidy profit these last 25 years.

"It was on her last voyage, on the first night out of Hamburg, that the first officer went missing. I knew nothing of this, of course, until the vessel came into the docks. By the time I got down there the police had spoken to the crew and Wade and Baldomero had been taken up. Wade is a youngster, little more than a boy. Baldomero is in his thirties, half-Spanish and half-stupid as I can make out. No one seems to know what happened and all the evidence is circumstantial, so what the truth of it may be I can't say.

"What brings me here, however, is this report which I have read in the paper.' He handed me a cutting from the *Courier,* neatly cut out and folded. 'I read here,' he said, 'that the men were sent for trial at the Assize, that the trial begins next week, and the case is to be heard in England because the murder was committed on the High Seas in a British vessel."

"Quite correct," I said, "for a British ship counts as British soil and the Queen's writ runs wherever the vessel may sail."

"And what if the vessel is foreign?"

"Why then, the men could not be tried here, for the court would have no jurisdiction."

"Now will all this be gone into at the trial?" he asked. "Must they prove she was a British ship before the case goes further? Shall I be summoned as a witness?"

"Well," said I, after a moment's thought, "The Crown must prove the *Sunrise* was a British ship but that will not be difficult for the harbour master will simply depose that the vessel was flying the red ensign when she docked. You will not be a witness and unless the prisoners know of your partnership with Mrs Müller it is most unlikely to be mentioned."

"Well I am heartily glad of that," he said, "for if the truth comes out, both Verity and me will lose our ship and all for a piece of paper in London that counts for nothing with me.

"Mind you," he added, as an afterthought, "there is a slip of paper which would count for something. When

we first started old Hubblecroft drew up a letter by way
of a partnership agreement which Verity and me both
signed over a sixpenny stamp. Of course I never told him
about the false declaration but I suppose he will still have
the document tucked away somewhere in that old coffin
room of his. Maybe I should ask him to send it over to
me, out of harm's way?"

'Then I told him that Hubblecroft had retired and sold
his practice, and that you, Bellamy, were taking it over
that very day.'

"And who is Mr Bellamy?" the Captain asked me.

'I told him that I had not yet met you, and knew only
that you had served your articles with a respectable
London firm and were highly spoken of as a very con-
scientious young man.'

"Oh, young Mr Valiant-for-Truth no doubt!" said
McKinlock. "I don't want him looking out my papers
that's for sure, so I think we will let sleeping dogs lie.
Now tell me what is your fee for this consultation and I
shall settle up directly, for I am going abroad myself in a
few days' time and can't say when I shall next be in these
parts."

"One moment," I said. "More than your ship is at
stake here. These two men are to stand trial for their
lives, but a word from you would set them free, for if the
registration was unlawful the *Sunrise* is not a British vessel
and the men must both be discharged. I think you bear a
heavy responsibility in this matter, Captain McKinlock."

"Stow that!" he cried. "The first officer was an Englishman, I am an Englishman, and Verity Müller is the

nearest thing to an Englishwoman you will find the world over. I'll not set these men free on a lawyer's quibble. They can stand trial before a British jury and I could wish for no better myself. Now mind, I have your word that this will go no further; no-one must hear of it, and especially not Mrs Müller." Then he paid my fee and left without another word.

'Well, gentlemen, I cannot say I was easy in my mind, but of course the matter was out of my hands. I had promised secrecy and the Captain was a man of mature judgment. So I resolved there was nothing further to be done.

'The following week Wade and Baldomero were tried at the Assizes. The case lasted two days and was reported in the *Courier*. The evidence was circumstantial, just as McKinlock had said, but such evidence can be very powerful and seemed to be so in this case. There was no witness to the deed and no body was found but it was believed the dead man had been thrown overboard and the men had said and done things which left little doubt of their guilt. They were both convicted and sentenced to death but for the younger man, Wade, the jury recommended mercy. He was only nineteen and could certainly expect a reprieve.

'They had both been defended by an eminent barrister, whom I have known for many years. It so happens that I have briefed this gentleman myself, for a case in the Queen's Bench next term, in preparation for which we had a consultation in his chambers last week. I took the opportunity to ask him privately about the *Sunrise*. I gave no hint of what I knew but only asked him if he thought the verdict a just one.

"I do not" he said, "and on the day the verdict was returned I sat up all night drawing a petition to the Home Secretary. It comes to this; that the young man is a handsome fellow who made a good appearance and spoke up from the dock, so the jury took a liking to him and recommended him for mercy. The Spaniard was some years older, surly and silent, with a villainous appearance and the jury took against him. Yet I believe the evidence against him was much weaker. Wade was the true villain and he led Baldomero on. A petition was got up, and Wade is already reprieved. Alas! For Baldomero I see no hope of a reprieve and no hope of a successful appeal, for the case raises no point of law."

'We talked about the case, and the more we talked the more troubled I became. It occurred to me that Captain McKinlock knew nothing of this, yet his decision could not be recalled. If I wrote to Mrs Müller she would surely deny any interest in the vessel. Also, time was running out, for the date of the execution had already been fixed.

'By this time, Bellamy, you and I had already met, for I had paid you a courtesy call soon after my meeting with Captain McKinlock. But how could I ask you to join me in a search through Hubblecroft's papers? You are a young man, at the outset of your career. Was I to propose, within days of your arrival here in Woodbridge, that you and I should conspire behind Hubblecroft's back to breach his client's confidence? No, if my solemn promise to Captain McKinlock was to be broken the responsibility must be mine and mine alone.

'For two nights I hardly slept as I turned the question over and over in my mind until I was nearly sick with the worry of it. Then I made my resolution. *Fiat justitia ruat coelum:* let justice be done though the heavens fall.

'There was only one way I could act without compromising your position. I should have to steal the Captain's papers like a common thief. It would not be difficult to manage. I knew the layout of your office, and especially Hubblecroft's cabinet room, in which he took such satisfaction. As to the breaking in, I had sat for many years as the Clerk of the Peace to the Borough Quarter Sessions and had seen many an old lag standing in the dock. I knew their ways and had learned their methods, though I little thought I should need to turn that knowledge to my own advantage.

'I went over to Bury St Edmunds and purchased a bolster in an ironmonger's shop where I should never be known. Then I made myself a door wedge, and waited until last Sunday morning when all good citizens would be in church. I walked round to the back of your office, carrying some legal papers of my own in case I should be surprised. I saw the upper window was open but I am no longer a young man and did not trust myself to climb on to the roof so I forced the door with my persuader, wedged it shut, and went upstairs.

'I am not made for thieving gentlemen, and I can tell you that my heart was beating and the sweat stood out on my brow as I thought of the terrible consequences if I should be caught in the act. But as luck would have it, all was quiet. I made my way into the cabinet room and found one of the mahogany boxes was labelled *Mac*. In there were no more than a dozen sets of papers, all tied round with pink tape in the usual way. It was the work of a moment to find the backsheet endorsed *McKinlock & Müller, 1870* with just a handful of letters and the partnership agreement the Captain had spoken of. I thrust the whole into my own file of papers and shut up the cabinet.

'I had not quite finished yet, but some instinct made me glance into the smaller front room, just by way of a precaution. There to my horror, Bellamy, I saw your bed made up in the corner of the room.

'The mind works in strange ways, especially when we are overwrought. No sooner did I see the bed than there flew into my head the dread phrase *breaking and entering a dwellinghouse at night* – the old definition of burglary at common law, so much more serious than mere housebreaking for it carries penal servitude for life and is only tried before the red judge on Assize. Indeed, in my father's time men were hanged for this very crime. Now I too had broken into and stolen from a place where a householder slept – in law, a dwellinghouse. Of course this was Sunday morning, in broad daylight, but my crime would not be discovered for twenty-four hours and who was to know, then, what time of day or night I had entered?

'My first thought was to stop the clock on the mantelpiece, but I realised at once that was foolish. If I stopped the clock at twenty minutes to twelve who was to say, when the clock was found, whether that was morning or night, or whether the time had been altered. Then it was that I saw the shaft of sunlight on the mantelpiece, and hastily scored the place where the shadow fell, to show at least that I had been there in daylight.

'It remained to leave the money I had brought, to compensate you, Bellamy, for the damage to the back door and a little over for your trouble. I wanted to leave a note about the mantelpiece, for the mark had gone rather deeper than I intended, but I could not write with a pen for fear my hand might be recognised. I saw your typewriter on the table, with a piece of paper inserted. I have never used such a machine myself but it did not seem to be difficult so I simply struck the letters and hammered out my note. The whole business had lasted no more than five or six minutes, and soon I was out of the building and walking back here to my own office.

'When I had leisure, in this room, to examine my booty, I saw at once that it disclosed the true ownership of the *Sunrise*. By noon on Monday I was with an Under-Secretary at the Home Office and laying the case before him under the seal of secrecy which I myself had so shamefully broken. There is less than a week in hand now before the execution but I am given to understand that my information will probably be decisive in the man's favour and the Home Secretary will recommend a reprieve. At all events, I have done what I could to spare the life of a fellow creature.

'Now I live in dread of the consequences. The authorities are in full possession of the facts. The *Sunrise*, I fear, will be seized and Captain McKinlock will discover that I have betrayed my solemn promise of professional secrecy. I have been a gentleman in the law for forty-three years and now I am utterly disgraced.'

'Unless of course,' said Holmes, 'Baldomero should happen to be reprieved, like Wade, on compassionate grounds alone with no further reference made to the ownership of the vessel.'

'Indeed, but how can I hope for such a thing, now that I have laid the facts before the authorities?'

'I am not without influence in certain quarters and it may be possible to reach a satisfactory arrangement.'

'If you could do so, Mr Holmes, I should be for ever in your debt. But you are not obliged to help me. Mr Bellamy is your client and he has no reason to think kindly of me, for I have brought this trouble upon his head.'

'You have indeed put me to a great deal of trouble Amwell,' said Bellamy, 'but I understand why you acted as you did. If the matter can be kept confidential I shall bear you no ill-will, I assure you.'

'Thank you for that,' said Amwell, 'and thank you also, Mr Holmes and Dr Watson. I am quite at a loss to know how you found me out, but no doubt you have your own professional methods.'

'You betrayed yourself, Mr Amwell,' said Holmes. 'It was obvious to me that Mr Bellamy's intruder was a man well versed in the arts of burglary but who was not a burglar by trade. No professional burglar leaves a cour-teous apology and a handsome gift for the householder he has robbed. Nor does he abandon the door wedge which is one of the tools of his trade. The intruder was careful to leave evidence that he had been present in the hours of daylight, a fact of particular significance in the case of a dwellinghouse. That showed a working knowledge of the criminal law. The sundial, improvised on the spur of the moment with the tools which came to hand, showed a quick and resourceful intelligence. The money left, ten guineas, was a sum which would most readily occur to a professional man, and one who could afford to lay out such an amount. All these matters were suggestive of a criminal lawyer, rather than a common criminal.

'I was convinced that something of importance had been taken, yet the premises had not been ransacked. An intruder in your own room, Mr Amwell,' said Holmes, glancing about him, 'would have the greatest difficulty in finding any particular document, but our intruder foresaw no such difficulty, for he knew Mr Hubblecroft's methodical ways. That suggested a local man, with particular knowledge of the practice.

'He was unlikely to have been young and agile, for such a one would have noticed the open window of the cabinet room and scrambled up over the flat roof. A middle-aged or elderly intruder was more likely, especially since he was unfamiliar with the use of a modern typewriter. The letters in your note of apology had been struck erratically, some heavily, and some in a light or tentative manner, a sure sign of the inexperienced typist.'

'You are quite correct,' said Amwell. 'As I say, I have never used such a machine before and never wish to again.'

'These observations,' said Holmes, 'sufficed to show that I was looking for a local solicitor who was no longer a young man. In addition to his criminal practice he was probably a property lawyer, since he had fallen into the habit of contraction which is peculiar to that class of practitioner. A conveyancer would naturally write *mr* for *matter* just as he would write *trees* for *trustees*.

'This much was a matter of scientific deduction from the known facts. I still had no notion of the motive for the theft but it must have been a strong one and I had no reason to doubt the reference to a matter of life and death. I then had a piece of good fortune. A minute examination of the mantelpiece showed a small mark on the wallpaper a little to the right of the deep sundial scratch. That smaller mark exactly corresponded with the width of Mr Bellamy's steel ruler. It showed that the line had been drawn against the left edge of the ruler, which would have been natural enough for a man holding the bodkin in his left hand. A right-handed man would have gone the other way about, holding the ruler in the left hand and the bodkin in the right.

'I now had most of the information I needed to identify the culprit. Dr Watson kindly agreed to scrutinise your supper club while I went to London and researched the professional history of every practising solicitor in Woodbridge. When we compared notes this morning there was little room for doubt. Your words when we entered this room sufficed to confirm my conclusions.'

After a long silence Mr Amwell said quietly, 'I suppose

Inspector Foulcher must now be informed.'

'Every point I have mentioned Inspector Foulcher has seen for himself. I have made certain deductions, but he has a theory of his own and since nothing has been concealed from him I think we may safely leave matters as they stand.'

'May I be told,' said I, reading from Holmes's card, 'what is *24 & 25 Vict cap 96, s. 1*?

'It is a reference,' said Amwell, 'to the definition section in the Larceny Act, 1861. I looked it up while you were waiting outside my room. It defines the hours of darkness for the purpose of burglary. As soon as my eye fell on that section I realised that the purpose of my sundial had been discovered, and that any attempt to deny my crime would be useless.'

* * *

Shortly afterwards we made our departure, Bellamy and Amwell shaking hands warmly, the latter not without a certain glistening in his eye. A few minutes later Holmes and I were on the train again, speeding back to London.

'I think I will leave you to go ahead to Baker Street,' said Holmes.

'Whilst you call into the Diogenes Club for a word with your brother Mycroft?'

'You know my methods, Watson.'

THE ENDELL STREET MYSTERY

ALTHOUGH rumours had been abroad for some months, it was not until the latter part of 1883 that the public learned the full details of Doctor Kennelly's disgrace at the hands of Kitty Lummis and the Blackfriars ring. At the time, of course, the credit for this successful investigation was accorded to Scotland Yard, but the true facts were undoubtedly known to the Home Secretary and certain other members of the cabinet. As I recall, the newspapers were still regaling their readers with the evidence in that case when we had our first consultation with the estimable Mr Royston Hatto.

Mr Hatto came to our comfortable rooms in Baker Street at the end of a late November afternoon. The weather was horrid. Mrs Hudson had drawn the curtains, turned up the gaslight, and lit the fire, but we could still hear the rain beating against the windows and the muffled sound of the cabs and four-wheelers trotting down to Marylebone while the pedestrians splashed their way home through the puddles.

None of this seemed to trouble our client who was shown up, prompt to the minute, and strode into the room with a broad smile on his face. He was a diminutive man in his middle fifties, with twinkling blue eyes and a huge black beard which would not have been out of place in a man twice his size. He was respectably dressed and to all appearances in the best of health, but he had lost his right arm and the empty sleeve was pinned into the pocket of his coat.

'Good evening Mr Hatto,' said Holmes, who was in his most affable mood. 'Let me introduce my friend and colleague Dr Watson. Now, pray pull your chair up to the fire and tell us about your case. Has it any connection with the terrible accident which cost you your position with the Bank?'

At this our visitor, taking his seat, gave a hearty laugh. 'Now, Mr Holmes,' he said, 'your reputation goes before you. I have heard of your trick of taking a man's measure at a single glance. Indeed,' he added, more seriously, 'that is the very reason I have come to consult you. But first you must tell me how my own appearance says so much about me, for I know I gave nothing away in my letter.'

'Elementary,' replied Holmes. 'Even in this weather the faint aroma of camphor tells me that your frock coat has been brought out of retirement for the present interview. Yet you yourself are in the prime of life. The coat is well worn, but is still a comfortable fit and by no means dilapidated. For some time, I suppose, you wore it every day, but then for some reason, left it off and have had no occasion to replace it. What that reason might have been is suggested by the shine on the elbow of your empty sleeve, and your letter of introduction. Your handwriting is that of an educated man, but slow and irregular. Like that of Lord Nelson it shows at what pains you have learned to write with the left hand after the loss of your right. I infer that you purchased the coat when you were in regular employment and had the use of your right hand. But the loss of your arm occasioned the loss of your situation, since when you have had little use for formal dress during the day.'

'Good!' said Hatto, with a broad smile; 'very good! But why an accident? And how do you find out my profession?'

'Your rude health suggests that you have recovered from an injury rather than a debilitating disease and that, as with Dr Watson, it was your wound which pensioned you off. As to your occupation, I see that although your coat is well worn the cuffs are still remarkably good. That at least is true of the left cuff, which I can see, and I will wager that the right cuff, which is pinned out of sight, is much the same. When I recall that linen cuff protectors are seldom worn with a frock coat, save by gentlemen in the City who spend their working day counting and weighing gold and silver, I deduce that you could have had but one occupation.'

'Capital, capital!' said Hatto; 'just what I had been hoping for – and perfectly correct in every respect. In point of fact I was the chief cashier of one of the oldest and most respectable banks in the City, the Liverpool London & Levant, in Throgmorton Street and I had worked there for 34 years, man and boy, when I had my accident. And now,' he said, settling back in his chair, and pausing for a moment, 'I must tell you how that happened.

'It was on a Tuesday afternoon when we had a quiet spell, and my assistant at the next position was counting out some sovereigns. A young man walked in – a customer as I assumed at first – stepped up to my assistant and threw a handful of pepper in his face. Then in an instant he jumped on to the counter, grabbed a handful of coins, leaped down again and made a run for it.

'I was after him in a shot and caught up with him just outside the main doors where I flung him to the ground. He kicked and struggled like a madman but I held on tight and shouted for help. Suddenly he twisted his head round and bit my thumb so hard it went right through to the bone. Oh how I yelled with the pain! But I still kept hold of him and in a moment two of the younger men were with me. Between the three of us we held him down until a police officer came running over from the Bank of England, blowing his whistle, and then our man was well and truly captured.

'I was very shaken of course, and my thumb was bad, so I was taken off to St Bart's where the wound was stitched and dressed and they gave me a mug of tea and sent me home.

'At first I thought I should soon be back to work, and none the worse for my adventure but the wound was very troublesome and turned septic. They did all they could for me, but in the end the surgeon told me that gangrene had set in, and was well advanced, and there was nothing to be done but amputation. So I signed the consent form that night and when I came round the following morning my arm was off.'

'Is this possible, Watson?' asked Holmes.

'I have known of such cases,' I said, 'but usually when

the wound has been neglected for some time.'

'Well, I suppose I was at fault there,' said Mr Hatto, 'for I should have gone back to the hospital sooner; but I kept telling myself it would all come right in a little while, so perhaps I paid the price for my own neglect. But I did have the satisfaction of knowing that my attacker had been convicted at the Old Bailey and sentenced to seven years with hard labour so I resolved to make the best of a bad job.

'No sooner could I sit up than I set about learning to write with my left hand. The Bank was still paying my salary, and one of the directors had called to see me in hospital, so I had some hopes of getting back to work again. Three months to the day after the robbery I presented myself in the director's office and showed him the progress I had made. I was a little nervous but I wrote a few ledger entries on a piece of paper and passed it across the table.

'The director was quiet for a little while and then said,

"I'm sorry, Hatto. It won't answer. Half your work, you know, is making up the ledger and for that we must have a hand which is neat and regular. Yours was the best in the hall but now it is like a spidery schoolgirl's. I feared as much, and am sorry to disappoint you, but we can't keep your position open any longer. However," he added, "you must not be downhearted. You lost your arm looking after our money, and we mean to see you all right.

"The fact is, the Board would like to set you up in business on your own account – in a small way, you understand, but with capital enough to earn you a respectable living; to rent and stock a small shop or something of that sort."

'Well you can be sure, Mr Holmes, I jumped at that opportunity and I knew at once the type of business I should go for. You see, it was our policy at the bank that we always gave our customers a fair rate of exchange for foreign money; not just for bills and notes, like some of our competitors, but also for foreign coins, however small and peculiar. It might be anything from Russian kopeks to Tibetan trangka, and all manner of coins and tokens from the Far East. But whatever the coin we always gave credit for it in the regular way. Of course there was no profit in this for us, for the coins could hardly be sent abroad again, but it built up our goodwill, and gave us a reputation for fair dealing.

'I had always taken an interest in these foreign coins, and used to exhibit some of them from time to time in a little cabinet in the entrance to the hall. In this way, over the years, I became quite knowledgeable, and began to build up a small collection of my own. I am a single man, you see, and this became my hobby at home, as well as part of my work.

'So I said I thought the Bank's offer a very handsome one, which I should wish to accept, and that I should like nothing better than to rent a little shop off the Strand or the Charing Cross Road and set up as a dealer in coins and medals. Well to cut a long story short, that was agreed upon. I found a little place near the top of Endell Street, opposite the Swiss convent, and a few weeks later

I opened for business. True to their word, the directors gave me the capital I needed, and also a great quantity of foreign coins which had been sitting in the strong room for years, so I got off to a good start, and soon built up a steady little business.

'All went well until four weeks ago, on a Thursday afternoon, when a young woman came into my shop. She asked to see some coins, and was not particular as to what type, so I gave her one of my rummage boxes, that is a box full of mixed coins, all priced at a penny, which my customers can pick their way through for anything which takes their fancy.

'One moment,' said Holmes, who had been listening with his eyes half closed and his long fingers pressed together; 'can you describe the woman?'

'She is no longer a girl, if you understand me, and her face is a little careworn, but she is still a good-looking creature. I am sure she has a French accent, but she says so little I find it hard to place her. She has no wedding ring, she is dressed very plain, and by her manner I think she must be in service, or she may be a shop assistant, or something of that sort.'

'Pray continue.'

'She spent an hour or more sitting at the end of the counter and going through my box, in a very methodical way. Now and again she would choose a coin that took her fancy, and put it to one side but – here's a peculiar thing – some two or three she thrust away from her with a little shudder, not putting them back in the box, but pushing them right to the back of the counter, as if they gave her the horrors.'

'Did you happen to notice what coins they were?' asked Holmes.

'I am sorry to say I took no particular notice,' said Hatto. 'They cannot have been very remarkable, or I would not have put them in with the others at a penny each.

'At all events, she eventually chose about twenty coins, mostly Indian exotics, scalloped and with holes in the centre, which I let her have for eighteen pence, and off she went. It was only a small purchase, and I was happy enough to serve her, but there was something about her manner which made me a little uneasy. She was fidgety and uncomfortable, if you understand me. And here is another odd thing; she only had one glove. It was a black leather glove, and when she came into the shop she put it on the counter beside her. Then when she left, she took it with her, but only carried it between her fingers, and never put it on.'

'Was this an item of fashion perhaps?' I asked; 'something carried for the sake of appearance, even though the other glove had been lost?'

'Oh no,' said Hatto, 'it had a particular purpose, of that I am sure. You see, just out of idle curiosity I stepped to the door of the shop and watched her as she left. She walked across to the convent and waited there for a moment or two and I thought she might go in. But then she turned on her heel and walked up the road towards St Giles. She had gone just a short distance when she looked about her, then stood over the gutter and shook something out of her glove. I could not see what it was exactly, but I thought it was some sort of powder.

'At once my suspicions were aroused. Why, I thought, this woman is a thief. She has had something in that glove, pepper, or worse, and has been waiting her opportunity. If I had slipped my guard she would have thrown it into my face, then grabbed some of my coins and made off with them, just like the ruffian who had tried to rob the Bank. And my first thought was, that I should not let her into the shop again.

'The next Thursday, you can be sure, I was on the look out, and just about the same time in the afternoon she came up the street. At once I put up my closed sign, bolted the door, and stepped into the back parlour. A few minutes later I looked to see if the coast was clear, and there she was, standing outside the shop and waiting for it to open. By now it had come on to rain quite hard, and she had no umbrella, but still she stood there, waiting patiently for me to open up.

'Just then one of my regular customers walked up and knocked on the door, so of course I had to open up for him. When I did so the young woman said, "Oh good! You are open after all", and stepped right in. It was foolish of me, I know, but she looked so drenched I had not the heart to turn her away. Then I saw she had the black glove with her, and at once she put it on the counter just as before. So I asked her directly, "Why do you have only one glove?"

"Now," she said, with a little smile, "I have been very particular not to notice your missing arm, and I should take it kindly if you would not mention my missing glove."

'At that my other customer laughed, and said, "That puts you in your place!" so I said no more about it and felt a little foolish.

'Once again she stayed for an hour or more, spent eighteen pence on some coins which had taken her fancy, and left when the light began to fail. She took the glove with her but this time I did not see what became of it as she ran down the street in the rain and was soon out of sight.'

'One minute,' said Holmes; 'did she, on this occasion, thrust some coins away from her?'

'She did indeed, just a few, but again with that little shudder, as if she could hardly bear to touch them. Well, to continue, the third week – that was last Thursday, she came again, and all was exactly the same, with her single black glove on the counter, some coins chosen, and two or three thrust away. I was watchful all the time but she was quiet and pleasant enough, and by the time she came to leave I thought my fears must have been groundless.

'For all that, I kept my eye on her when she left the shop. Once again she stood outside the convent for a minute or two, turned round, walked a little distance down the road, emptied her glove into the gutter, and walked off towards St Giles.

'Well, then my head was all in a whirl, and I thought, perhaps I am wrong to trust her after all? What if she has an accomplice? It might even be the same man who robbed the bank seven years ago and will now be at liberty again. Has he tracked me down to take his revenge? He would have the advantage of me now, for I could never fight him off with one arm.

'That night I thought the matter over and the next day I went to see Inspector Maddison of the City Police who had prosecuted the robbery case for the Bank. I told him of my fears but he said this was now a case for the Metropolitan Force, as my shop is outside the City limits. He referred me to Inspector Lestrade at Scotland Yard, who offered to have a constable on duty outside the shop for two or three weeks. But I thought, that will never do, for word would soon get round that I had something to be afraid of and my regular customers would be likely to stay away.

'When I explained this to Mr Lestrade he said, "Then why don't you consult Mr Sherlock Holmes, for he likes anything out of the ordinary and may be able to advise you better than I." To tell you the truth gentlemen, I believe he thought me something of an old woman, and perhaps I am, but I can't afford any trouble for the shop is my whole livelihood now.

'Well that is the state of the case, and my hope is, that you may be able to step down to my shop tomorrow afternoon, just for five or ten minutes, to take a look at this young woman and tell me what you think. You can tell so much at a single glance I am sure you will be able to say whether she means me any harm.'

'You may be hoping for too much,' said Holmes. 'Given half a minute I can generally tell a woman's occupation or fortune, and something of her history. But her intentions are a different matter altogether. I have to confess that I once spent twenty minutes in the company of an elderly milliner without the least suspicion that she was to drown her husband the following day.

'Besides, I regret to say that tomorrow is quite out of the question. I have another investigation on foot which demands my presence in Limehouse tomorrow afternoon, and probably for most of the night. How are you situated Watson?'

'No better than yourself' I replied, 'for McAlister is out of town tomorrow and I have undertaken to look after his patients, one of whom is in a very bad way.'

'Ah well,' said Hatto, 'It is such short notice and you are both very busy men; perhaps next week would not be inconvenient?'

'We need not wait till then,' said Holmes, for this I fancy is a job for the Baker Street irregulars: one in particular, Wiggins by name, a young man of remarkable promise. You shall make his acquaintance in due course, Mr Hatto. Let us meet again at the same time on Friday and see what he has to report. In the meantime, be cautious, but do not turn the lady away. Be good enough also to put on one side any of the coins for which she seems to have a particular revulsion.'

*   *   *

Two days later the weather had taken a turn for the better and the air was crisp and dry. Mr Hatto returned, and was once more shown up to our room.

'Mrs Hudson,' said Holmes, 'you may now bring up

young Wiggins from the back kitchen and we shall hear what he has to report.'

A moment later the young man appeared. He was, as I remembered him, a typical London street arab, ragged and none too clean, but with the lively intelligence of the true cockney. He stood in the centre of the room and was not in the least abashed as the three of us turned expectantly towards him.

'I done what you said, Mr Holmes,' he said. 'I saw the lady go in the shop, then kept out of the way for an hour or so until she come out. Then I give her a just a few yards, walked up with me big eyes and said,

"Got any foreign coins lady?"

"What do you want them for?" she said, in a funny sort of voice.

"To take 'em round the bank lady, and get some money for 'em."

"You won't take them into that shop will you?"

"Not likely – he won't give me nothing for 'em."

"Very well" she says, "you can have these."

'Then she reaches into her pocket, and gives me a little handful; and here they are Guv'nor,' saying which he handed over his little treasure, which Holmes immediately passed on to Hatto.

'Why!' said Hatto, 'These are the very coins I had sold her just before she left the shop. She gave me a shilling for them, only to give them away to this boy, who must have been a stranger to her. I don't like the look of this, I must say.'

'No more do I,' said Holmes. 'What happened next

Wiggins?'

'I pushed off sharp, but kept an eye on her, and just like you said, a little way up the street she emptied out her glove. So I waited till she was off out of it, then went up with your envelope Guv'nor, and picked up a little bit of the powder – and here it is,' saying which he handed over a very grubby envelope with as much care as if it had been the Crown jewels.

'Well done Wiggins,' said Holmes, 'Your help has been invaluable. You must leave the coins with us, but here is a florin for your trouble, and you may ask Mrs Hudson to give you a good supper before you depart.'

'One moment,' said Hatto, 'I too must show my gratitude. Here are two shillings more, and an Indian rupee for good luck.'

'Much obliged to you Guv'nor,' said Wiggins, and a moment later he was rattling down the stairs to his supper.

Holmes carefully opened the grubby envelope, studied the contents, then moistened the tip of his little finger, dabbed it in the powder, and tasted a morsel on the tip of his tongue. 'Common soot,' he said, 'scraped from the back of a fireplace, and perfectly harmless. Now Mr Hatto, were there any coins this week which sent a shudder down the lady's spine?'

'Just these three,' said Hatto, handing them over. 'Two five-centime pieces from the second Empire and a Danish eight-skilling piece of 1871.'

'And now, we must see the coins she gave to Wiggins.'

Holmes spread the two lots of coins out on the table,

and turning them over from time to time, seemed lost in thought for a few minutes.

Eventually Hatto broke the silence, by asking, 'What do you make of it Mr Holmes?'

'You may set your mind at rest on one point,' he replied. You have nothing to fear from this woman.'

'Then you think she is harmless?'

'On the contrary, I believe that she does indeed have an accomplice and they are set upon some desperate crime, robbery perhaps, or even murder.'

'But you said I had nothing to fear!'

'Because you are not her intended victim. Consider – she has no interest in you or your coins. She could have robbed you half a dozen times already, had she a mind to. No, she is using your shop as a place to wait and watch. Before she comes to Endell Street she takes care to fill her single glove with a quantity of soot. All the time she is in your shop she keeps it by her, ready to use at a moment's notice. But when she leaves the shop she has no further use for it. It is troublesome and incon-venient to carry about and she disposes of it. However, the following week she goes to some trouble to procure a fresh supply of soot.

'What is it for? Hardly for self-defence, since she only expects to use it in or near your shop – a shop whose stock-in-trade holds not the slightest interest for her and from which she could, if she wished, stay well away.

'Conversely, as a weapon of offence it is more or less harmless. A handful of soot may disconcert a man for a few moments, but little more. But that might be time enough to distract her victim and for an accomplice to strike home, perhaps with a lethal blow.'

'I cannot believe she is intent on murder,' I said.

'Any yet I suppose you have no other explanation for her sinister behaviour?'

'As you have often remarked, Holmes, it is a mistake to theorise on insufficient data.'

'*Touché* Watson! A hit, a very palpable hit! Well, I will endeavour to renew Lestrade's interest in the case, but I have little hope of any action from that quarter. In the meantime, Mr Hatto, let us lay our plans for next Thursday on the supposition that your mysterious lady will appear once more. I think you mentioned that you have a small back parlour?'

'Yes indeed.'

'Large enough to accommodate a pair of auctioneers' clerks, taking an inventory of a particular collection?'

'In the guise of Dr Watson and yourself,' said Hatto, with a smile; 'By all means.'

*   *   *

Holmes and I arrived in Endell Street soon after midday the following Thursday. It was, and is still, I believe, one of those quiet backwaters which are sometimes to be found, even in the very heart of London. At the upper end of the street was the dignified and slightly forbidding frontage of the Swiss Convent. Directly opposite, next to a small brass foundry with its shutters up, was Mr Hatto's shop. This, we were surprised to see, was a former tobacconist's and the large mirrors behind the counter, advertising Havana cigars and ship's tobacco were still in place.

'You did not mention these mirrors, Mr Hatto,' said Holmes, thoughtfully. 'Would I be right in thinking the young lady generally sits here, at this corner of the counter? Yes? Then, without turning her head she has a clear view of the buildings on the other side of the street, especially the convent, which is directly opposite.'

'Is that important?' asked Mr Hatto.

'It may be highly significant,' said Holmes, 'or quite immaterial. It is too early to say. We must wait upon events.'

We soon installed ourselves in the back parlour with two large notebooks in which we sat diligently writing. We could hardly be seen from the shop, but for the sake of good form we had a collection of coins in front of us which, from time to time we turned over and examined, as if we were indeed preparing a catalogue. In fact I was writing up some notes of an earlier case and Holmes was working on some abstruse mathematical formulae. The work was not unpleasant, since in the best traditions of the Liverpool London & Levant Mr Hatto had taken care to provide us with refreshments in the way of sherry and biscuits.

From time to time a customer would come into the shop, which seemed to be doing a brisk trade, and after about an hour the mysterious lady herself appeared. We could hear at once that it was she, from Hatto's tone of voice but the woman herself spoke so quietly and so briefly that we could hardly pick up more than a word or two.

Shortly afterwards Hatto put his head into the parlour and said, quite loud enough to be heard, 'How are you getting on gentlemen? Do you need anything more?' To this we made some reply and then heard him explaining our presence to his customer, so as not to alarm her.

It was about an hour later when we heard Hatto say, 'Have you chosen what you want?' and guessed that the young woman was about to leave. This was my cue, as we had previously arranged. I stepped out of the back parlour and had my first opportunity to glance at the lady. I saw that Hatto's description of her had been very accurate, and he had not been unkind in describing her as 'careworn.' I thought myself she had a hard face, which was emphasised by the way she had pulled her hair back in a bun. But I had no time to linger as I walked through the shop, remarking that I was going to look out for a cab. Then I stepped across the road and waited on the opposite kerb, looking up and down, as if I expected a hansom to appear at any minute, and knowing that if by any chance one did arrive I should have to temporise.

I was standing in front of the convent. The street was very quiet as dusk began to fall but just a few feet to my left a priest, in a black cassock, was speaking to a well-dressed, middle-aged man. The man appeared to be seeking directions to an address which the priest did not appear to recognise. Hardly had I noticed them when the young lady stepped out of Hatto's shop, walked across the road, and passed in front of me. She was carrying her black glove and, to my astonishment, as she passed the priest, she slapped it against the front of his cassock, spilling a quantity of soot over the garment. Then she continued on her way, without so much as breaking her step.

The priest swung round, with some annoyance, made some remark to express his irritation, and began to brush the soot from his front with the palm of his hand. Then the stranger, who had been asking directions, spoke again, but now his voice was harsh and steady.

'Show me your hands,' he said.

The priest looked at the man, then glanced down at the sooty palms of his hand with an air of bewilderment.

'Show me your hands,' said the man again, and then, when the priest did so, '*Poudre.*'

There was a moment's pause, and the man said again, slowly and distinctly, '*Poudre.*'

The effect of the word, when repeated, was electrifying. In a moment the priest's face took on a look of abject terror as, with a sudden realisation of his peril he turned and fled for his life. A voice from the other side of the street cried, 'Watson!' but it was too late for me to intervene. At the very instant when the priest, stumbling on the skirts of his cassock, fell to the ground a shot rang out, and a moment later he was writhing with pain in the gutter.

'Watson! Look to the priest!' cried Holmes, as he confronted the assassin, but the man was not to be taken. Levelling his revolver at Holmes from only a few yards away he let off two more shots, so that my friend was obliged to take cover in a doorway. That was all the man needed, for it gave him a head start and he ran off towards the maze of little streets which converge on Seven Dials, where a man can be lost from sight in less than a minute.

I ran over to the priest, and knelt beside him on the ground. He had lost some blood from a wound in his left shoulder, but I could see at once that it might not be fatal. Looking up I saw two Sisters of Mercy who had evidently emerged from the convent when they heard the gunfire and were ready to give what help might be needed.

I told them I was a doctor. 'Shall I send for an ambulance?' asked one, 'Or a policeman?'

'No! No!' cried the priest, in a strong French accent; 'no ambulance, no police. Just take me inside.'

We did so, for he was able to walk, leaning heavily on my arm. In this way we helped him into the convent, and through a long dark passage to a small infirmary at the rear of the building. Here we were able to lay him down, still whimpering with pain, on an iron bed. One of the Sisters brought a blanket, some disinfectant, and a kidney bowl with a scalpel and one or two other instruments. I was about to probe the wound with one of these when a young woman's voice behind me asked, 'Will he live?'

I turned to see Holmes, Hatto, and the young woman, whom Holmes was holding firmly by the arm.

'Yes,' I said, 'he will live.'

'As you see Watson,' said Holmes, 'I missed the father but had the good fortune to discover the daughter, who could hardly tear herself away from the scene.'

'He was not my father.'

'Come, madam,' said Holmes, 'the resemblance is striking and he is twenty years your senior – if not your father
then certainly your uncle. Has someone sent for a constable?'

'No! no!' cried the priest again from his sick bed: 'No
police! No police! I shall press no charges.'

'Then we shall have to conduct our own investigation,'
said Holmes. 'Watson, when you have attended to your
patient, you may care to join us on the other side of the
passage.'

My patient detained me for no more than twenty
minutes, in which time I had found, and extracted the
bullet which had lodged between the left scapula and
clavicle. I debrided the wound and, with the Sisters' help,
applied sutures and a large dressing and bandage. When I
was satisfied that for the time being there was no more to
be done I stepped into the next room where Holmes and
our client were patiently waiting with their prisoner.

The room was like the vestry of an old parish church;
homely, untidy, and lit now, as the light began to fail, by
a single gasolier in the centre of the ceiling. Holmes and
Hatto were seated at a small table, and the young lady sat
on a bench facing them. For the first time I was able to
study her face, once beautiful perhaps, but now distorted
by fear and anger.

'And now,' said Holmes, 'you will be good enough to
explain why you and your accomplice attempted to
murder the good priest.'

'The good priest!' she echoed, with a bitter laugh. 'Hell

is too good for him!' She was excited now, and her French accent was more pronounced.

'That is as good as a confession,' said Holmes, 'but before I go further I wish to know not what you did, for that I saw for myself, but why you did it. Your motive madam, if you please.'

'I have nothing to say,' she said in a voice which at first seemed calm and controlled. But a moment later her emotions overcame her, and she began to sob quietly, with a sort of hopeless despair.

Holmes gave a exclamation of impatience, but I held up my hand and when the woman began to recover her composure it was Hatto who asked her, 'What is your name, my dear?'

'Madeleine Lasalle.'

'I advise you to be candid, Miss Lasalle,' said Holmes. As yet we know nothing of your case, and until we know the truth we cannot tell how to act for the best.'

At this the woman gave a deep sigh, and looking from one to the other of us, with tears in her eyes, began to speak.

'I was born in Nantes, but brought up in Paris by my father, who was a civil servant. I never knew my mother but I had a younger sister, Adèle.

'In 1870, when the war broke out, I was eighteen and my sister only sixteen. Oh the excitement! The marching regiments with their dark blue tunics and scarlet pantaloons, the bands playing, the cuirassiers trotting past with their breastplates glinting in the sun! Everyone said, in six weeks time we should be marching into

Berlin.

'But the rest, you know; we suffered a terrible reverse, the Army was routed and Paris was besieged. At first we still clung to our hopes; every day balloons were sent up from the courtyard of the Gare du Nord, and there was talk of a great sortie by the National Guard. But when at last the sortie came it was driven back and then our hopes withered. The truth was, we were encircled and defeated, and that too, in the dead of winter.

'We had little enough to eat at first, and as the weeks went by we lived with hunger every day. Towards the end my father was able to buy some zebra meat from the zoo, but that was soon gone and then there was nothing but black bread and the sewer rats which we bought from the street vendors for two francs apiece, and boiled in an evil-smelling stew.

'In January we capitulated and the Prussians marched down the boulevards in triumph. That was bad, but worse, far worse, was to follow. The Emperor had abdicated, and the National Assembly signed an armistice, but the National Guard, and the people of Paris would have none of it. They seized the Hotel de Ville, ran up the red flag of the Commune and pulled down Napoleon's column in the Place Vendôme. Then came retribution and the terrible week of blood. The National Assembly sent the Army into Paris, with orders to suppress the rebellion. In the very face of the enemy, Frenchmen began to kill each other.

'My sister had a sweetheart, Paul who was in the National Guard, though little more than sixteen himself. He had fought the Prussians at Buzenval and now he threw in his lot with the communards.

'For a week or more he and some others, some National Guardsmen, some students, mounted guard on the barricade at the end of our street in the district of Belleville. When the battle came Paul stood his ground and fought with the best of them, but in less than half an hour it was all over and the Army had prevailed. Three of the communards lay dead, several were wounded, and some had fled into the houses. Then the soldiers came and turned us all out into the street, to stand alongside the men they had already taken captive. My father was in Montmartre, on some urgent business, but Adèle and myself, waiting anxiously for his return, were rounded up.

'In the end there were about seventy of us. We were told to stand with our backs against the wall. The soldiers stood in line directly opposite, watching us silently, with their weapons loaded and their bayonets fixed. In the distance we could hear the sound of gunfire which told us there was still fighting in other parts of the city.

'A party of soldiers, led by a young officer, was walking rapidly along the line of captives. As they came along they pulled out most of the younger men, and some women, sending them under guard to the other end of the street. It seemed the ones they picked out were the ones who had been fighting. Yes, some of the women had been fighting, I cannot deny it. Some had served the guns, some had been firing from the windows and one was said to be an arsonist, one of the *petroleuses,* who were feared and hated most of all.

'There was no screaming or shouting. The people were sullen and fearful. Only some of the children who had been left in the houses were crying. We were only a few yards from Paul and he worked his way round to where Adèle and I were standing. A rumour went round. Someone said, "The ones they take are for the prison at La Roquette, or the stables at Versailles."

'Then I heard Paul say quietly, "Their orders are, to take no prisoners."

'By now the officer's party was only a few yards away. Paul turned to Adèle, grasped her hand, kissed her cheek, and said, "Goodbye my love; vive La France!"

'Even as he spoke I saw how the officer and his party were proceeding. As they passed down the line the officer was saying "Show me your hands." Of course a communard who had been firing a musket, or a rifle, would soon have a smudge of black powder or grease across the top of his hand, and probably on the side of his face. For this officer a glance at the hands was enough to condemn a man. If the hands were clean he said nothing. But if he said "*poudre*" the man was instantly taken away.

'All this took less time than I have taken to explain it, for they set about their dreadful task with all speed. By now they were almost upon us and then, with a thrill, I recognised the officer. His name was Torrance – Emile Torrance. We had been to school together, his father knew my father, and I had even been to his home. I knew that he had joined the Army two years ago, but since then I had seen nothing of him.

'Emile!" I cried; "it is me, Madeleine! Madeleine!" but all he would say was, "Show me your hands".

'My hands were clean, but Oh horror! Adèle's were black, where young Paul, fresh from the smoke of battle, had clasped them just moments before. On her cheek too, was a smudge, where he had kissed her.

"*Poudre!*" said the officer.

"No! No! Emile!" I cried, "She is innocent! This is my sister Adèle. She is only sixteen! You cannot take her! You cannot!"

'But they took her, Monsieur. They took that pretty young girl who had no part in the war, and no part in the Commune, and had never harmed them or any living creature. As they took her she called my name, and one of them struck her with the butt of his rifle to silence her.

'I called to Emile again, as he continued on his way. I beseeched him to spare her. But he would not. Instead he turned and looked over his shoulder at me. He recognised me I know, and on his face was scorn and contempt. He knew Adèle was innocent, just as I did, but he had it in his power to destroy her and he chose to do so.

'Soon they had gone down the line, and taken all they wanted. Paul and Adèle, and the rest, twenty or thirty of them, were led away to a small side street, while some of the soldiers remained to guard us. Then the shooting started. When I heard the sound of the rifles I thrust my fingers in my ears. But I could not shut out the screams; they will remain with me to my dying day.

'It seemed to go on for an eternity, but I suppose it

was no more than ten or fifteen minutes. Then the soldiers sent us back into our houses, under curfew, and on pain of death, and began to demolish the barricade. I never saw my sister or her sweetheart again.

'That night I broke the news to my father. He had been away for only a few hours and in that time his happiness had been destroyed. I told him too of Emile, the brave "Lieutenant Torrance" who that night would stand his friends a drink and tell them, with a laugh, how he had finished off my sister.

'In that dark hour, gentlemen, my father and I – yes, it was my father – swore a dreadful oath. We swore that we should have an eye for an eye and a tooth for a tooth; that Emile Torrance would die, and die in terror, in the dreadful knowledge that he had brought his fate upon himself.

'All this was for the future. For the moment we had only to flee Paris, which we did a few days later. After a few months, when it was safe to return, I enquired after Torrance, but could learn only that his regiment had been posted to Algeria.'

'It is no wonder,' said Holmes; 'that the coins of the second Empire, with the head of Napoleon III, should arouse such revulsion in you; indeed it seems you can hardly bear to touch any coin whose date reminds you of the dreadful year of 1871.'

'Spy!' said the woman, turning her flashing eyes on Hatto.

'Better a spy than an assassin,' said Holmes, dryly. 'When did you learn that Lieutenant Torrance had left the Army and taken Holy Orders?'

'Only six weeks ago, and only by chance. My father and I came to England in 1875. I have lived and worked here ever since. I am in service in Hackney and Thursday is my half holiday. My father is sometimes in England but more often abroad. Where he is now I cannot say.

'Six weeks ago, when I went to mass, our usual priest was absent for some reason. Imagine my horror when I saw in his place, officiating at the altar, Emile Torrance. I knew him at once. Twelve years could not erase the memory of that evil man; and now, *mon dieu!* he is a priest; a cruel, cold-hearted murderer, elevating the Holy Sacrament.

'I left the church at once, and later found out all I could about him. I learned that his usual duties were in Westminster, and that he was sometimes in attendance at this convent, but always left before evensong.

'That was enough for me, and for my father. We knew what had to be done, for we had spoken about it many, many, times. For four weeks we made our separate ways here, taking care to exchange no more than a glance, but waiting the opportunity which we knew would come. Four weeks! I would have waited forty, if need be, or four hundred, to see the look of terror on his face when he heard the word "*poudre*".

'The rest you know. I regret nothing.' Then she added, with a bitter laugh, 'I have done nothing. What is the punishment, in this country, for spilling a little soot on a man's garment? Shall I be required to pay his laundry bill?'

'Do not prattle,' said Holmes; 'on your own confession you conspired to murder him.'

'So you say, but he will never give evidence – the coward. You heard what he said, "No police!" I have nothing to fear from such a man.'

Just then there was a knock on the door, and one of the Sisters appeared and after a word of apology to us spoke briefly to the girl in French.

'He wants to see me,' she said, 'alone.'

'Do you wish to see him?' I asked.

'I am indifferent. I might see him, just for a moment, to please the Holy Sister.'

'Are you to be trusted, Madam?' asked Holmes, sternly.

'Of course. I have no weapon. He will come to no harm.'

'Then you go and see him, my dear,' said Hatto.

She nodded and followed the Sister out of the room. I expected her to be gone for no more than two or three minutes but as we sat in silence the minutes slipped away. It was nearly half an hour later when she returned and stood for a moment in the doorway of the room.

'Well madam?' said Holmes.

'If he is not under arrest, he will leave England within the week and will never set foot in France again.'

'You threatened another attempt on his life.'

She shrugged. 'I told him the choice was his.'

As to what more had passed between them she would say not another word. Nor would Torrance when I retur-ned to the infirmary to make sure he was still comfor-table. The Sisters assured me they could care for him there for a day or two and I could see that he was in good hands.

Before we left, Holmes, Hatto and myself took a moment to confer in the dim corridor outside the little room where Madeleine Lasalle was still sitting.

'Mr Hatto,' said Holmes; 'I think between us we have resolved the little problem with which you presented us. It is for you now to decide how we should proceed. Torrance's silence will not preclude a prosecution, for we saw with our own eyes what transpired and we have all three heard the woman's confession.'

'How badly is he hurt Dr Watson?' asked Hatto.

'He has had a lucky escape,' I replied; 'had he not tripped and fallen at the very moment when the shot was fired the wound might have been fatal. As it is, in the Sisters' care he will be up and about soon enough, and little the worse for his experience.'

'And what of her father Mr Holmes? Is there any chance of catching him?'

'Very little,' said Holmes, 'unless we keep a strict watch on the daughter. I have no doubt he will lie low for a few days until they can meet in safety. He will, of course, be travelling under an assumed name, and indeed the name she has given us may well be false.'

'Then I propose we do nothing,' said Hatto. 'Let the girl go home, let me shut up my shop for the night, and let you gentlemen return to Baker Street, with my best thanks.'

We were, of course, happy to follow our client's advice. As we sat in front of the fire that evening, and Holmes was filling his pipe after supper, the conversation turned once more to the Commune, and the dreadful year of 1871, when the finest city in Europe was in flames, disfigured by violence and betrayal.

'Do you suppose,' I said, 'that Emile Torrance has begun to repent his sins?'

'Let us just say, Watson, that it is not unknown for a bullet wound in the shoulder to change the course of a man's life, for better or worse.'

THE DORSET WITCH

IN the winter of 1891 my friend Sherlock Holmes was as busy as ever. In the space of a few weeks he had rescued the celebrated Madelaine Vansittart from the custody of Archdeacon Braun and exposed the true nature of the Scientific Bicycle Company. His chemical experiments often kept him up late into the night and he had been asking my advice about a curious case of spontaneous combustion in Venezuela.

Such was his capacity for work, however, that he was always glad to see a client who presented a novel or interesting problem. One such visitor was Mr Oliver Gladwell who called by appointment on a bright November morning. It had snowed overnight and some boys were throwing snowballs in the street. Mr Gladwell presented an easy target when he stopped to ring our doorbell and had spent a minute or two brushing himself down before he was shown upstairs.

This little incident had given our visitor a rather apologetic appearance. He was middle aged, slightly built and quietly spoken. He stooped a little, wore spectacles and when he spoke occasionally stroked the air gently with his hands.

'Mr Holmes, Dr Watson, I have come to see you on the recommendation of Mrs Hudson,' he said, 'who was sure you would be able to help me. As you see we are

neighbours,' he said, as he presented his card and grate-
fully took a seat by the fire. 'I am the proprietor of a
small hotel, the Waterford, at number 187 Baker Street.'

'Not so small, I think,' said Holmes. 'Twelve bedrooms,
three bathrooms, a writing room for commercial travel-
lers and an excellent chef who served for some years in
the French navy. You keep two carriage horses in the
mews at the rear and a brass plaque in your entrance hall
suggests that Prince Jerome Napoleon was a guest in
1867.'

Mr Gladwell gave an apologetic little cough and said, 'I
was not aware you had stayed with us, Mr Holmes.'

'I have not had that pleasure,' said Holmes, 'but my
profession encourages the habit of close observation.
And now, Mr Gladwell, you must tell us how we can
help you.'

Our visitor hesitated for a moment before beginning
and then said, 'I take it, Mr Holmes, that you do not
believe in witchcraft?'

'On the contrary,' said Holmes. 'When the victim is
ignorant or superstitious witchcraft can be a very potent
weapon. I know of two cases which were fatal and a third
in which the victim was only saved by the last-minute
intervention of a priest.'

'Oh dear! I do hope you don't come to see me as ignorant or superstitious.'

'Let us hope not. And now the facts, if you please.'

'I should first explain that the hotel is very demanding
of my time and in consequence I am rarely out of
London; not often, indeed, away from Baker Street.

However, last week I had occasion to go down into Dorset. It happened in this way. My parents are no longer alive. My late mother had a younger brother, Mr Roland Ballentine of Old Hall, Dorchester. I knew him only slightly and we last met many years ago. There was no estrangement, you understand. It was just that distance and the passage of time kept us apart.

On Monday of this week I had a telegram from a firm of solicitors to say that my uncle had died and his will named me as the sole executor. I must say this came as a surprise. I don't believe he had ever asked if I would be willing to undertake that duty and it is frankly not one that I welcome.'

'In which case, said Holmes, 'you are not obliged to do so. An executor may always decline to act.'

'So I understand,' said Gladwell, with that peculiar gesture of stroking the air, 'but it seems there is no one else prepared to take on the estate so I suppose I shall have to make the best of it. At all events, when I read the wire I took the train down to Dorchester and put up at The Antelope. As you may suppose, being in the hotel line of business myself I soon fell into conversation with the proprietor. He told me what he knew of my late uncle who apparently was a well-known local character. He had a reputation as a man with a short temper and a very colourful turn of phrase. He had never married and kept only a small household; a cook, a housekeeper and three or four other servants.

'The housekeeper, I learned, was a wild Irish woman with flaming red hair who was said to have some hold over my uncle. The locals called her Black Molly. She was said by some, only half in jest, to be a witch who kept a familiar; a black cat to which she spoke only in Gaelic and which sometimes changed shape into a little dwarf with only one eye and a blue face. This was all nonsense, of course: the sort of nonsense country women like to talk, but my host found it amusing and I must confess my curiosity was aroused.

'The following morning I met the solicitor who had telegraphed me and was shown my uncle's will. It was made about two years ago. There was a small bequest to myself as executor, similar bequests to the servants and two or three modest legacies to personal friends. The residue of the estate had been left to the Aldgate and Whitechapel Mission for Female Unfortunates. I say, "had been left" because there was a codicil made just three weeks ago, when my uncle must have known that he was dying. The codicil left the original will unchanged except that the residue was now left to the housekeeper, Mrs Mary O'Sullivan – the same Black Molly I had been told about the night before.'

'Has the estate been valued?' I asked.

'Not yet, but Old Hall is a substantial property and well kept up. Mrs O'Sullivan will be left in comfortable circumstances. However, the solicitor suggested, given the unusual features of the case, that both the will and codicil should remain confidential until they are formally read to the assembled company after the funeral.

'When I left the solicitor's office I found a trap to take me over to the hall. It is an old house, built in the reign of Queen Anne and sits well back from the road a mile or two out of town; rather out of the way in other words. There was black crepe on the door handle and the blinds were drawn and the place had a rather gloomy aspect but the furnishings are comfortable and, as I say, the house is in remarkably good order.

'It was the cook who answered the door and she took me through to meet the housekeeper who has her own room. Mary O'Sullivan was sitting in a rocking chair. She was, as I had been told, a woman of striking appearance; still slender and handsome but no longer young. Her red hair hung lose but she was dressed in full mourning and spoke with a strong Irish brogue. I noticed she had a clay pipe at her side although she did not venture to smoke it while I was there. Indeed, she hardly stirred from her chair during my visit but seemed to be watchful and suspicious. In point of fact, I don't believe she took her eyes off me until I left the room.

'I introduced myself and began to explain the purpose of my visit. "So you're the nephew," she said, "and it's a fine nephew you are that never saw the man for twenty years nor set foot in the house. But you're here soon enough to see me out on the street."

'I protested that I came to see her in good faith and had no wish to put her out of the house. I tried to explain that my mother and Mr Ballentine had never been close but had been content, each of them, to go their own way. I added that the will was to be read after the funeral and that until then I was not at liberty to disclose its contents.

"You need not trouble yourself, Mr Executor," she said, "for I know all about the Female Unfortunates and aren't I unfortunate myself?"

'Our conversation continued for a few minutes in that vein. I noticed that, for a domestic servant, she had an unusual and extravagant turn of phrase. At one point she said, "Sure, I am buffeted like a raven in the wind" and later, "The anger of the Lord will come upon us."

'She did in fact have a black cat which at one point wandered into the room and she spoke to it in what I took to be Gaelic – it was certainly not English. As she spoke I could see her looking at me directly as if she was hoping to vex or puzzle me.

'I did not prolong my visit, thinking I could return to discuss matters of business a day or so later when the good lady would have had time to compose herself and come to terms with what the future might hold.

'In the meantime I had to engage a house agent to view the hall and make an inventory of the furniture. This took a day or so to arrange and it was not until yesterday that I returned to the hall, with the agent, hoping, perhaps to get on better terms with the housekeeper. The visit went quietly at first. It was the cook who showed us over the house and we took notes as we went from room to room.

When we came to Mrs O'Sullivan's room I took great care not to cause offence, by asking her permission to enter and promising to stay for no more than a minute or two. As we went in I noticed something which I must have overlooked on my first visit: a broomstick propped up against the fireplace – an old-fashioned broomstick like a gardener's besom.'

'Or a witch's broomstick,' said Holmes dryly.

'Just so. The room was not large and as the agent was stepping past the fireplace I picked up the broom and moved it to one side. Black Molly – Mrs O'Sulivan – positively screamed at me. "My broomstick!" she cried. "My broomstick! Don't you dare touch it. It's nothing to you! Leave it be, I tell you! Leave it be!"

'I was quite taken aback, as you may imagine. "Please," I said, "I meant no harm. I shan't touch it again."

'"No harm indeed!" she said, with a sort of grimace. Then, looking me straight in the eye and speaking most distinctly she said, *May your horses stumble and your eyes grow dim with weeping!*

'Did she know you kept horses?' asked Holmes.

'How could she? We had never met.'

'That was a tremendous curse,' I remarked. 'The Irish certainly have a way with words. You must have been hard put not to smile.'

'On the contrary, she spoke with such vehemence that I was rather unnerved and, as I shall explain, I have little cause to smile. The agent attempted to reassure the woman but she was in such a state of excitement that there was nothing more to be done. We left almost at once, after making arrangements with the cook to see that the immediate needs of the household were cared for.

'As we left, Black Molly was waiting in the porch and accosted us again. "It's all mine", she said. "The house, the garden, the furniture. All mine. You shan't see a penny of it."

'So as you see, it was hardly a satisfactory visit. I came back to London last night but I have to go back to Dorset on Monday for the funeral.'

'But clearly something more has happened since you returned,' said Holmes. 'Has the witch's curse taken its toll? Have your horses stumbled?'

'Worse than that! Call it superstition if you will, but as soon as I arrived home I went down to the stable to look at my horses. One was lying on the stable floor, flailing about. The other was still standing but sweating heavily and swaying from side to side. The stable boy was there and a groom from next door and they were doing what they could, but to no avail. The first horse died within the hour and the second did not survive the night.'

'I am sorry to hear it,' said Holmes. 'This must be a heavy loss.'

'It is indeed. They were fine hackneys and cost me about seventy pounds. I was very fond of them and made a habit of visiting the stables every morning.'

'What do you know about the diseases of horses, Watson?'

'Less than I could wish,' I said. 'My patients go on two legs and horses have ailments and vices all of their own.'

'And then of course, Mr Gladwell,' said Holmes 'there is the question of your eyes.'

'I beg your pardon?'

'I take it you have not been weeping over this affair?'

'It has certainly set me back, Mr Holmes, but no, I

have not actually wept.'

'Yet in the few minutes you have been in this room you have twice taken off your spectacles to rub your eyes and on each occasion you have looked thoughtful and troubled. Black Molly said your eyes would grow dim and you are secretly fearful that her prediction might come true.'

'Oh no,' said Gladwell, stroking the air again, 'Now you do think me foolish. My eyes are giving me a little trouble just at the moment but that is nothing to do with Black Molly I am sure. Dear me, no.'

'I am glad to hear it and if you need reassurance I am sure Dr Watson will be more than happy to examine you.'

Since I knew exactly what was troubling Mr Gladwell I was relieved when he made it clear that he did not wish to become one of my patients. To change the subject and make light of the matter I asked, 'Did you see anything of the blue-faced leprechaun with only one eye?'

'I have not yet seen him but I believe he is flesh and blood and that he called at the hotel in my absence. My manager tells me that an individual of that description was asking after me on the very day I went down to Dorset. The man's appearance seems to have been quite grotesque and it was evidently a very brief visit. He declined to leave his name or any further details and left as soon as he learned I was not at home.'

'Could this singular visitor have had access to your stables?'

'Very easily. He had only to walk down a side street to

the mews at the rear.'

'Do you suspect foul play?'

'I do hope not but I seem to have made at least one enemy and until today I did not believe I had an enemy in the world. Also,' he added, stroking the air again, 'today is Friday the 13th, which is always said to be un-lucky.

'Mr Holmes, Mr Ballentine's funeral is on Monday and the purpose of my visit is to ask if you would be good enough to come down with me and be present when the will is read.'

'I am a consulting detective. I specialise in crime. There are some interesting features of your case but, leaving aside this nonsense about witchcraft, I am not clear how I can help you.'

'I want to be sure that everything is above board: that – if you will forgive the expression – there has been no skullduggery or underhand dealing. I did not welcome the executorship but since I have undertaken it I mean to carry it out thoroughly. In particular, I wish to know whether Black Molly is truly entitled to the bulk of the estate or whether such a forceful woman may have bullied or tricked my uncle into changing his will.'

'That is surely a question on which the solicitor can best advise you. He must have seen your uncle when he made his first will and again when he signed the codicil. No doubt he will have formed an opinion of his own.'

'You have not met Mr Sillitoe. He is a charming gentle-man of advanced years and no doubt perfectly com-petent in his own way but I don't believe he has an enquiring mind. In short, I think he would prefer to let sleeping dogs lie. Of course, it may be that my misgivings are without foundation. I certainly hope so. But I don't care for mysteries and I want to see this particular mystery cleared up.'

'Very well. As it happens I am free of engagements next week. If all goes well I could travel down by train on Monday morning and be back in Baker Street in time for a late supper.'

'Splendid!' said Gladwell. 'I am most grateful to you. I shall go down on the Sunday night and stay at the Antelope again so we can meet up there.'

'What an extraordinary case!' I said as I stood at the window and watched our client hurrying back to his hotel with his collar pulled up against another volley of snowballs. 'Witchcraft, no less, complete with a witch's broomstick and a witch's curse!'

'And a gullible client who is old enough to know better.'

'You are a little too hard on him. He did not ask for all this trouble but he is clearly honest and determined to act for the best. Besides, it will be a kindness to Mrs Hudson to oblige someone she introduced to us. At all events, what do you make of his little mystery?'

'There is very little mystery about it,' said Holmes. An old man dies, an old woman is irascible and our client's eyesight is troublesome. These are disconnected events which Gladwell has persuaded himself are in some way related. He is frightened of shadows. However, I should like to know why his horses were suddenly taken ill.

'I shall have to go down to Dorset, of course, but it's probably a fool's errand and I can hardly ask you to waste your time as well as my own.'

'I should like to come, nonetheless,' I said. 'At this dreary time of year a day or two out of London is always welcome and I have some sympathy for Mr Gladwell in his predicament.

'By the way,' I added, 'I think it was tactless of you to mention that his eyes were troubling him. You saw that he was embarrassed by the remark.'

'Why so?'

'Because he did not care to mention the obvious reason which is the abominable state of the air in this room. You forget, Holmes, that you and I are acclimatised to strong tobacco, a coal fire and the pungent smells from your latest chemical experiments. For a visitor the combination can be quite overpowering.'

'I will bear that in mind, Doctor,' said Holmes, with a dry chuckle.

*   *   *

Holmes left before breakfast the following morning and I saw nothing of him until the middle of the afternoon. Then the door opened and a man walked in whom I first took to be a groom or ostler. He had a florid complexion and was wearing a tweed jacket with britches and gaiters, a cloth cap which had seen better days and a scarlet kerchief at his neck. Add to that a distinctive gait, half way between a saunter and a swagger, and I could see at once that this was a man who spent his working life in the stables.

As usual when he resorted to one of his many disguises it took me a moment or two to recognise my friend. Then I cried, 'Good heavens, Holmes! I thought we had another visitor. You have been working on a case – our neighbour's case I suppose?'

'Give me five minutes to change and I will put you in the picture.'

He soon returned in his dressing gown, filled his pipe and stood with his back to the fire.

'Where have you been?'

'In the tap room of the Horse and Groom and the public bar of the Turk's Head in both of which I gained a wealth of information, none of which was of the slightest use to me. It was not until the Pontefract Castle that I struck gold.'

'A hard day's work!'

'A long day, certainly. But if you wish to learn your neighbour's most intimate secrets there is no substitute for a few pints of ale in a public house.'

'What have you learned?'

'Gladwell's horses were poisoned.'

'Poisoned! By whom? The curious gentleman with a blue face and only one eye?'

'As to that, there is a conspiracy of silence; a conspiracy to which, from motives of gallantry, I have for the moment subscribed.'

'Gallantry!' I cried. 'And you have often said that poison is a woman's weapon.'

'Indeed so,' said Holmes, with a smile which made it

clear that there was no more to be said.

Early on the Monday morning we took the train from Waterloo. The weather had cleared since Mr Gladwell's visit and the air was crisp and bright as we rattled down through the beautiful countryside of Dorset, the bare branches of the trees outlined in the open fields against the sky.

We met our client as arranged in the coffee room of the Antelope Hotel where he introduced us to the solicitor he had mentioned: Mr Sillitoe, an amiable, grey-haired old gentleman who appeared to be a little hard of hearing.

'What can you tell us about the late Mr Ballentine?' asked Holmes.

'Interesting man,' said Mr Sillitoe, who had a rather clipped way of talking. 'Remarkably tall and fit. Hunted with the South Dorset for many years. He could be irascible, of course. He told me as a young man he was stage-struck. He used to go to the theatre every night when he was in London and wanted to go on the stage himself. I think he did secure one or two small parts at the Haymarket and Drury Lane. But his height was against him. Made him too conspicuous. The leading men don't care to act with someone so much taller. So he had to give it up in the end. But he always had a theatrical way of talking. Loved to quote Shakespeare. When he wanted to consult me about his will, for example, he said, "Come let us sit upon the ground and tell sad stories of the death of kings."'

'And he consulted you, I believe,' said Holmes, 'shortly before his death?'

'Consulted me twice, in fact. The first time was about two years ago when he made his first will. That was curious. He was quite clear in his mind about the small bequests he wished to make to his servants and so forth and equally clear that he wanted Mr Gladwell to be his executor. But he seemed uncertain what to say as to the residue of his estate.

'I urged him to consider some charitable bequest. As it happens I keep a list of charities to which clients of mine, over the years, have left money. I showed him the list. He glanced at it, pointed to the first name and said, "That's as good as any." The list is in alphabetical order so the first name happened to be the Aldgate and Whitechapel Mission. That's how they came to be named. I don't think there was anything more to it than that.'

'And then,' said Gladwell, 'three weeks ago he changed his mind and named Mrs O'Sullivan in place of the charity.'

'Indeed,' said Sillitoe. 'That was equally off-hand in a manner of speaking. Made an appointment to discuss the will. When he'd finished quoting Shakespeare and I asked for his instructions he just said, "Strike out the White-chapel Unfortunates! Expunge their name! Let them be anathema! Put in Mary O'Sullivan. It's all the same to me." So I had a short codicil engrossed and he came back the following day and signed it.'

While Mr Sillitoe was giving this explanation my attention was caught by a stranger who was sitting in the far corner of the coffee room reading a newspaper and smoking a cigar. He was middle-aged, very short, and very smartly dressed. As Sillitoe finished talking the stranger put down his newspaper and came across to speak to us. Only then did I realise that the poor man had suffered some terrible injury. He had lost the left eye and the socket had closed up into a hideous scar which covered almost the whole of that side of his face. The flesh around the scar was a sickly blue in colour and strongly contrasted with the other side of his face which was still clear, strong and handsome.

I think we all realised at once – I certainly did – that this could only be the man with the blue face whom Gladwell had told us about.

When he spoke his voice was quiet and cultivated and I detected a gentle Irish accent.

'Forgive the interruption, gentlemen,' he said. 'May I ask if you are here for Mr Ballentine's funeral?'

Gladwell and Sillitoe looked to Holmes who simply said, 'We are.'

'And may I ask, is Mr Gladwell one of your party.'

'I am,' said Gladwell.

'I called at your hotel last week, Sir, in the hope of meeting you, but you were away on business. This unhappy business, perhaps. Allow me to introduce myself. My name is Michael O'Sullivan. My mother is Mrs Mary O'Sullivan, Mr Ballentine's housekeeper and I have an interest in the estate.'

'I don't believe, Sir,' said Mr Sillitoe, 'that you are mentioned in the will.'

'Are you the solicitor dealing with the estate?'

'I am, Sir.'

'And may I ask who are these two gentlemen?'

Holmes, who had been studying the man's face in that careful way of his, answered at once. 'My name is Sherlock Holmes. I am a consulting detective and this is my colleague Dr Watson. Mr Gladwell has retained our services. May I ask what precisely is your interest in the estate?'

'I am one of Mr Ballentine's creditors. I will say no more for the moment but you may wish to speak to me before the will is read. Please forgive this intrusion. I will step into the next room now to give you a little more privacy,' saying which he picked up his silk hat gave a slight bow and moved away. As he did so I noticed that he walked with a pronounced limp.

'What a terrible injury to his face,' said Gladwell.

'Gunpowder,' said Holmes. 'Am I right, Watson?'

'Certainly,' I said, 'The colour of those pockmarks is unmistakable.'

'Yet he was never a soldier,' said Holmes, 'for he is less than five feet tall. A sailor, perhaps on a man-o'-war, for many sailors come home with a limp.'

'Seems deuced impatient for his money,' said Sillitoe. 'Bad form if you ask me. He ought to submit his account to my firm in the regular way.'

'He is not in need of money,' said Holmes, 'for he is a wealthy man. His hat came from Lock's of St James's and his cigar case from Comiot Frères in the Burlington Arcade. His tie pin cost thirty pounds and his watch chain not much less. He is evidently a gentleman, despite his grisly appearance.'

'I did not know,' said Gladwell, 'that the housekeeper had a son. She made no mention of him when we spoke – not that we had a very long conversation.'

'Nor a very civil one by all accounts,' I said, but hastened to add, 'Of course that was no fault of yours.'

'At all events,' said Holmes, 'we have found the little dwarf with a blue face and only one eye whom gossip says is the witch's familiar. Perhaps,' he added with a dry smile, 'he will turn into a black cat directly.'

We found time for a brief lunch and then had not long to wait before our four-wheeler arrived and we set off to the church for the funeral service. The congregation was a small one but Mr O'Sullivan was there and seemed to assume the place of the principal mourner. There was no sign of his mother whom I had yet to meet. It had turned bitterly cold with a chill wind and the internment in the churchyard was as dismal as such affairs always are. I was relieved when it was over and we set off for the hall where the will was to be read.

Mr O'Sullivan had preceded us and as we arrived was clearly in charge of the proceedings. He began by ushering Holmes, Gladwell, Mr Sillitoe and myself into a small library at one side of the entrance hall.

'Is this about your debt, Sir?' said Sillitoe, with some irritation.

'It is, Sir,' said O'Sullivan respectfully, 'and I will come to the point directly. Mr Ballentine's estate, this house and its contents and his personal effects, are worth together about eight thousand pounds. He is indebted to me for more than twice that sum. In short, he died insolvent, and when I am paid there will be nothing left.'

'Forgive me,' said Gladwell, stroking the air, 'this does not look like the home of an insolvent debtor. I was here last week and met your mother. The place is very well kept up.'

'With my money', said O'Sullivan. 'It's all underwritten by my loans and the loans are all evidenced in writing as Mr Sillitoe will be able to verify in due course. I am telling you this, not because I am anxious to be paid but because I do not wish the beneficiaries under the will to build up false hopes.'

'You are evidently not acquainted with its contents,' said Holmes.

'I am not, but I understand one of the metropolitan charities may have an interest.'

'No longer,' said Sillitoe. 'The will was changed. The main beneficiary is your mother. Otherwise there are just some modest legacies to the servants and two or three of the testator's personal friends. The total does not exceed a few hundred pounds.'

'Very well. I will undertake that those shall be paid in full.'

'You mean to say,' said Sillitoe, 'paid out of the estate?'

'There is no estate,' said O'Sullivan. He spoke quietly but in a very direct manner. That's what I am telling you. I shall pay the small legacies myself. For the rest, I shall suffer a heavy loss but since the loss is merely financial it's of no consequence.'

'I understand,' said Sillitoe, rather stiffly. 'I shall of course require documentary proof of your debt but for the moment let us proceed on the assumption that you are correct.'

We then passed into the main room where about a dozen individuals were already seated including the clergyman who had conducted the service. Mr Sillitoe, with the reassuring manner of a family solicitor, took charge of the proceedings, reading first the will and then the codicil slowly and carefully from beginning to end. He added that should there be any difficulty in funding the individual legacies Mr Michael O'Sullivan had undertaken to pay them out of his own resources.

He was heard in respectful silence. I had expected the revelation that Mrs O'Sullivan was the residuary beneficiary to occasion some surprise and I did indeed notice one or two significant glances when that section of the will was read. However, no comment was made and everyone seemed satisfied that the formalities had been dealt with in the proper way.

The company then retired to the adjoining room where some refreshments had been prepared. O'Sullivan once more took Holmes and myself on one side.

'I want you to meet my mother,' he said, leading us down a passageway to a room at the rear of the house. He knocked on the door and the three of us went in.

The room served as a sitting room and bedroom combined. It was comfortably furnished, the curtains were drawn and there was a fire burning in the grate. Black Molly, as I had come to think of her, was sitting bolt upright in her rocking chair. Mr Gladwell had been right to describe her appearance as striking. She was dressed in black from head to toe, her face was pale and her auburn hair had been tied up in a bun. Just as Gladwell had said, her eyes were watchful and suspicious. Her old broomstick was leaning against a dresser and a large cat was sleeping on the bed.

'Hello Michael,' said his mother in a strong Irish accent. 'Turn that way, so I can see the best side of your face. Did the funeral go well?'

'It all went very well, Mother, God rest the poor man's soul.'

'May the saints in heaven receive him. A good man laid to rest. And what company is this?'

O'Sullivan introduced us and she asked, abruptly, 'What's your business?'

'We came here to see justice done, Madam,' said Holmes, briskly. 'To hear the will read and to satisfy ourselves that everything is in good order.'

'I know all about the will', she said. 'All the money's left to the poor unfortunate women in London but I don't care for that because when Michael's debt is paid there'll be not a penny left over and we shall all perish.'

'You know very well you are talking nonsense, Madam,' said Holmes. 'Both you and your son appear to be in comfortable circumstances. There is a codicil to the will which names you as the main beneficiary and I have no doubt Mr Ballentine told you as much. Of course if you wish to pretend that you are hard done by you are free to do so.'

She ignored Holmes and spoke to her son. 'It is true, isn't it Michael? The money comes to us?'

'You know it is, Mother. My debts must be paid first but between the two of us we own the house and everything in it.'

'That's as it should be, Michael; as it should be.'

It was clear from the way the old lady looked hard at us that we were not expected to linger. O'Sullivan promised to speak to us again shortly, so we left and returned to the library. The whole interview had lasted no more than a minute or two but I shall long remember the remarkable scene, with the old lady in her rocking chair, her broomstick by her side, her black cat on the bed and her son with his face turned to one side to conceal his terrible scars.

We were standing with our client and his solicitor in the library when Mr O'Sullivan rejoined us.

'Your mother is a remarkable woman,' said Holmes, 'and no doubt you have been remarkably patient with her. You will now tell us, if you please, how she came to have such a hold over her late employer and how he came to be so greatly in your debt.'

'I will tell you the story now, gentlemen, just as my poor mother told me before I ran away from this house.

'I must begin many years ago. My mother was born in Ireland, one of dozen or more children living from hand to mouth in the back streets of Dublin with a drunken father and a broken down mother. It's a wonder she lived to be fifteen or sixteen – she has never known her proper – age but so she did, and took up with a soldier when she was hardly more than a girl herself.

'They were married, and the soldier nearly got a flogging for that because it was done without his officer's permission. For a few weeks my mother lived half in and half out of the barracks. You may guess what followed. There was trouble in the Orange Free State and the regiment had orders to sail for South Africa. On the day of embarkation all the wives had to come down to the quayside. Only a handful were allowed to sail with their husbands and they had to ballot for it just before the men went on board. My mother lost out and she never saw my father again, or knew what became of him.

'How she smuggled a passage to Portsmouth, shortly afterwards, I shall never know. Desperate times call for desperate remedies. But that is how she found herself in what was then, to her, a strange country, for she had never set foot in England before. She had no food and no money. She was carrying a child – myself – and the only English she knew was what she had picked up from her husband and the other soldiers.

'Now most of the Irish, in those days, made their way to London or Liverpool. But my mother's idea was to go west and she went on foot through the New Forest and down into Dorset. She was living from hand to mouth sometimes begging, sometimes working and sometimes starving. At last, when she was very near her time, she was taken into the casual ward of the workhouse here in Dorchester.

'Do you know what the workhouses were like, gentlemen, forty years ago? Grim, hard, unforgiving places and little better now for all I know. Well that's where I was born and where I should have died, I dare say, but for the kindness of two people: one I shall never know and the other was Mr Ballentine.

'It happened like this. Every year, in November, they used to hold a hiring fair in Dorchester. You will know this, Mr Sillitoe, and have seen it for yourself, I dare say for it's still done even now in a small way. The farm labourers and servants looking for work would stand in Cornhill, just off the High Street, and the farmers would come along and see who they wanted to hire for the following year. Now the idea was, if you wanted work you would put a ribbon in your hat and carry the tools of your trade. So if you were a shepherd you would carry your crook and if you were a carpenter you would carry a saw, and if you were a housemaid you would carry a broom.

'Well I was less than a week old, and not expected to live, I believe, when my mother got leave to go out of the workhouse for a few hours, in the hope of finding some employment. She asked for the loan of a broom but that was out of the question for fear that she might steal it or sell it.

'Her hopes were not high for she had to stand in the street in her workhouse uniform and nobody wanted a workhouse girl if they could have some one more respectable, with a good character. Even the other young girls at the fair stood apart and would have nothing to do with her. To add to her troubles, she had nothing to hold – not so much as a mop or a feather duster – so she had to stand there in her old-fashioned parish clothes more like a beggar than a servant looking for work.

'And that was where the first act of kindness came along. I said the other girls would not talk to her and so it was, at first. But one hearty young woman, holding a broom, was quickly taken up for a housemaid. She had found work within the hour. As she left she came across to my mother, gave her the broom – and a broken down old broom it was, even then – and wished her good luck. It was done so quickly that my mother hardly had time to thank her.

'The day wore on and my mother stood there holding the broom. By the end of the morning most of the hiring was done and the ranks thinned, as you might say. Pretty soon she was the only servant left: a starveling Irish girl with a borrowed broom and a tiny sick baby in the workhouse infirmary.

'It was growing dark when Mr Ballentine came by. I believe he had seen her from the coffee room of the Antelope; the very room where we met earlier today. I am sure he had no need of a housemaid but he understood her plight all too clearly. Many a time he had stood in line under the arcade in Drury Lane, hoping to be chosen as a 'super' or supernumerary in one of their big pantomimes and many a time, though he was near the head of the queue and had been waiting for hours, he was passed over. He had the same experience at Sadler's Wells and the Haymarket and the same hopeless feeling every time he was sent away empty-handed.

'I believe, indeed he told me so, that it was those memories which made him take pity on the poor woman. He walked over and spoke to her. He pretended not to notice her parish union clothes, took time to question her, explain the work he wanted and agree a fair wage. Then he gave her a shilling to seal the bargain and she agreed to start work the following day. She went back to the workhouse that night with gratitude in her heart for the girl who had given her the broom and the man who had given her some dignity.

'As to the silver shilling, I don't believe she had ever seen such a coin before; all she knew was pence and ha'pence. So from that day forward she would never part with it, nor with the broomstick. The coin was sewn into her purse and the broom was kept beside her bed for she said it had saved her life. It may be so, for she told me once that if she had not found work that day she was resolved to throw herself into the river.

'That is why, you see, the broom became a sort of talisman for her. She kept it close and could be very cross if anyone so much as touched it.'

'I can vouch for that,' said Gladwell. 'for I had curses heaped upon my head just for moving it to one side.'

'But, gentleman,' O'Sullivan continued, 'my mother had said nothing to Ballentine about her child. She had been terrified to do so. And when she left the workhouse the following morning she had to leave me behind. She prayed that all would be well with me and that her new employer would not find out her secret for she thought if he knew the truth she would be instantly dismissed.

'Little did she know Mr Ballentine. When he came to

hear of the child – which he did soon enough for gossip travels fast in such cases – he sent for my mother.

"What's this I hear?" he said. "You've an infant in the workhouse, born out of wedlock."

"That he was not," said my mother, trembling and tearful. "He's my lawful son indeed but his father's gone for a soldier and I don't know where. We are brought down by misfortune."

"Why," said Ballentine, in his flamboyant, theatrical way, "here is injustice! It must be remedied. The workhouse is the Devil's sarcophagus and the Guardians of the Poor are the Devil's henchmen. Fetch the child hither!" Those were his words, my mother said, and I don't doubt it for he had the most extraordinary turn of phrase.

'He was as good as his word. I was brought home the following day – for I count this old hall as my home – and was reunited with my mother. She brought me up here, and taught me to respect Mr Ballentine as our benefactor. But I saw little enough of him, especially when I was young, for he was often away on business and his business was often troublesome.

'Now being Irish, my mother had a good ear for language and by degrees she fell into the same theatrical way of speaking as the old man. She picked up some of his phrases and added plenty of her own. Indeed she was quite the equal of him when it came to imprecation and invective.'

'That, too, I can vouch for,' said Gladwell. 'My ears are still burning.'

'I was not a healthy child,' O'Sullivan continued, 'and had the misfortune to grow up as you see me: let us say not quite as tall or straight as my mother might have wished nor as grateful as I should have been. I was, I am sorry to say, a truculent and difficult boy and of course had no father to put me right when I misbehaved. When I was sixteen I ran away from home and tried to enlist. But the Army had no use for men with one leg shorter than the other and I had to find another way of making a living.

'After many adventures, and many a night without supper, I made my way to London and from there on to Essex for I heard there was work to be had in the gunpowder mills at Waltham Abbey. It was true enough and I was taken on at the factory gate; just as a casual labourer at first but I worked hard and soon had a steady job.

'I was a smart lad, though I say it myself, and I had a good eye for an opportunity. When the civil war came, in America, there was a great need of ball-and-paper cartridges for the Enfield rifles. I found I could make those very easily in my own lodgings and with a small outlay, so I set up in business on my own account. I made up the cartridges in boxes and sold them to a company in Limehouse which shipped them overseas. Then I rented a little shed, took on some young women to help me and soon had a thriving business.'

'Gunpowder is dangerous, of course, and accidents will happen, even in the best-regulated workshops. That's why you see me with a blue face and only one eye. But I count myself fortunate for it could so easily have been worse.

'I wrote to my mother, just now and then at first, to reassure her and then when I was established, every month. I always planned to visit her in Dorset as soon as I could get away from the business for a day or two but I held back after my accident because I knew she would be shocked by my appearance.

'When the civil war ended the cartridge business fell away so I went in for the larger explosives used by quarrymen and railway engineers and, to cut a long story short, my business prospered and I became a wealthy man.

'Then, some ten or twelve years ago, my mother wrote to me in earnest to say Mr Ballentine had fallen on hard times. I could put off our meeting no longer so I came over and was reunited with my mother. I had written to warn her that I had lost my good looks and my appearance went hard with her, I know. However, she bore it well and had her own fresh troubles for if Mr Ballentine had to sell up she would lose the only real home she had ever known.

'I saw Ballentine and came to the point directly. "I know that you are in trouble," I said, "but I don't know how this has come about."

"Alas!" he said, "When sorrows come, they come not single spies but in battalions."

"Never mind that," I said. "What has become of your fortune?"

'He told me then that he had been badly hit when Gurney's Bank failed. They had nearly all his money and although he had tried to economise his situation had grown worse year by year and his capital was nearly all used up. It had got to the point where he would have to dismiss the servants and sell the hall.

"How much do you need?" I asked.

'He did not care to tell me but I soon got it out of him. He owed nearly three thousand pounds. I had brought some money with me, knowing it would be needed, and I counted out five hundred sovereigns, then and there. A day or so later I gave him the rest of the money he needed. I have lost most of that, of course, but I don't regret it. One good turn deserves another.'

'You mentioned earlier a much larger indebtedness,' said Sillitoe. 'Further loans?'

'A dozen or more, mostly for small amounts, to a total of £19,050.'

'Including interest?'

'I have charged no interest and want none. That is the capital sum.'

'Evidenced in writing?'

For reply Mr O'Sullivan produced a small black memorandum book from an inside pocket and opened it at the first page. Mr Sillitoe studied this with a doubtful expression.

'Hmm!' he said. 'Just a list of payments with dates and initials. I would expect to see more than this. No promissory notes? No bills of exchange? No cheques cleared and returned by your bankers?'

'I never asked for a promissory note and I always paid in cash. It has always been cash with me. Cash on the nail.' And he added with a wink, exaggerating his Irish accent, 'And isn't that the secret of my success?'

'What do you make of this, Mr Holmes?' asked Sillitoe, handing the little book over to him. I expected Holmes to study the document in some detail, peering at it with his lens and turning it over and over as I had seen him do so often. Instead he gave the list of payments little more than a passing glance and seemed more interested in some of the memoranda on other pages.

'There are some useful formulae for explosives in this little notebook,' said Holmes. 'You should take care it does not fall into the wrong hands.'

'And the loans?' asked Sillitoe, adding by way of second thoughts, '*Alleged* loans? Is this a genuine document?'

'Undoubtedly. The entries were made at various times using various different pens: mostly steel pens but on the last two or three occasions a reservoir pen using blue-black ink. The list is untidy, the handwriting is poor and there is an error of addition on the second page which increases the total due by fifty pounds. It would not impress a judge or a revenue inspector, not least because each receipt should have carried a penny stamp but it was not written to meet the strict requirements of the law. Had Mr O'Sullivan wished to produce a forged document he would certainly have taken much more trouble over it.'

'Thank you, Mr Holmes, said O'Sullivan. 'The old man never asked for a stamped receipt when he gave my mother the first shilling she had ever seen in her life and I trusted him, just as he had trusted her.'

'Very good,' said Sillitoe. 'I rely on your advice, Mr

Holmes. We'll take out a grant of probate on Mr Glad-well's behalf and with Mr O'Sullivan's help the estate can be wound up.'

'What will you do, Mr O'Sullivan?' I asked.

'I believe I shall come and live here. It's a fine house and Dorchester is a very pleasant town. I can look after my mother and she can end her days here.'

'Mr Ballentine must have held your mother in high regard, Mr O'Sullivan,' said Sillitoe.

'You touch on a delicate point there,' said O'Sullivan. 'My mother worshipped Ballentine, as you may imagine. She looked on him as her saviour in this world, as indeed he was. However, her regard was not reciprocated. The fact is, Ballentine was not an easy man to please and in his later years especially I think he found my mother eccentric and vexatious. So she can be; who can deny it? I have fallen out with her often enough myself. Nor did he care for her habit of imitating his flamboyant speech. He thought it an impertinence. He never regretted helping her and he never once thought of sending her away but he did not enjoy her company.

'I have always thought better of him on that account. He was as kind to the cantankerous old lady as he had been to the helpless young woman. He was steadfast.'

'As you yourself have been,' said Holmes.

There was little more to be said. Leaving our client and Mr Sillitoe to discuss the business arrangements Holmes and I set off on our journey back to Baker Street. As dusk fell our train departed and we settled down to a comfortable journey.

'It is dreadful to think,' I said, 'that at one time old women were hanged or drowned for witchcraft.'

'Terrible indeed,' said Holmes. 'Yet our belief in witchcraft is no less foolish than the belief in unicorns or that in savage parts there were men whose feet were large enough to serve as umbrellas. The fact is, our fellow men like to think that they are rational creatures but they are easily frightened and often receptive to the most extraordinary ideas. Think of our client, for instance, half believing that his horses had been bewitched.'

'He is still in the dark over that affair and so am I. You would only say that O'Sullivan had nothing to do with it and that poisoners are often women.'

'I am too secretive, Watson. It is a fault of mine. My excuse is, that I was anxious to protect a young woman, hardly more than a child, who was in danger of losing her livelihood.'

'I would not have abused your confidence. Holmes.'

'Of course not, my dear fellow. But I gave a solemn promise to my informant that I would not reveal the girl's name until she was out of danger. She came from the Marylebone workhouse and was taken on two weeks ago as a kitchen maid in our client's hotel. She noticed how, every morning, Gladwell visited the stables and gave the horses a few lumps of sugar. When he went down to Dorset she thought they would miss their daily treat. She did not dare to steal any sugar from the kitchen but instead sneaked away and fed them some Galloway pippins which she had found in an outhouse.

Now, horses will eat all the apples they can get but nothing is worse for them. The girl found an ample supply and thought she was being kind and generous. Little did she realise the harm she was causing. All seemed well at first but the symptoms of colic came on rapidly and when the stable lad found her out it was too late to do anything.'

'And has he said nothing? Surely, Mr Gladwell should have been told?'

'To his credit, the lad has breathed not a word.'

'But the girl deserved to lose her place.'

'She has been brought up ignorance and poverty and like Molly O'Sullivan she deserves a second chance.'

'It is not like you to be sentimental, Holmes.'

'I suppose not. And yet when all other explanations have been exhausted the one remaining hypothesis must be correct. I have evidently been bewitched.'

THE OTTOMAN SALOON

A MONG my notes of Mr Sherlock Holmes's cases, and certain other papers, in my tin dispatch box at Cox & Co at Charing Cross, is a small packet carefully wrapped in linen and tied with pink tape. It contains half a dozen faded newspaper clippings, some old letters, and some other items including a delicate glass vial, about two inches long, with a cork stopper. None of these items has anything more than sentimental value, but such were the circumstances in which they came into my possession that I have never been willing to part with them.

In the winter of 1886 I was sharing lodgings with Holmes at Baker Street and our breakfast often coincided with the arrival of the post. Holmes, whose correspondence was far more extensive than my own, opened his letters rapidly, but invariably noticed the postmark and glanced at the back and front of each envelope before neatly slitting it with his Italian stiletto.

On one such morning the first envelope he opened produced a short exclamation followed by, 'What do you make of this, Watson?'

He showed me a small brass key, about two inches long, and of a rather old-fashioned appearance. There was a label attached, on which was written, in a sloping hand, 'Here we are again!'

'Does it come with a letter?'

'No, only this blank sheet of writing paper.'

'How very singular!'

'The envelope is equally curious.'

Holmes showed it to me. It was a stout manilla envelope. The address, widely spaced and written in pencil in a frail hand, was to 'Mr Shirlock Holmes, 221B BBaker Street, London.'

'Sherlock with an *i* and two *Bs* in Baker Street,' I remarked. 'Is this a practical joke of some kind?'

'I hardly think so,' said Holmes, 'but we must see if anything comes of it,' saying which he strode over to the mantelpiece and thrust the envelope and its contents into a rack with some other correspondence.

We had not long to wait for the next development. About a week later, shortly after six o'clock in the evening, an unexpected visitor was shown up and announced as Mr Gerald Tovey. He was a short, thickset man of middle years, clean shaven, his dark eyes clean and alert behind a pair of steel-rimmed spectacles. He carried his ulster over his arm and in his hand was the type of hat which in New Zealand, I believe, is known as a 'hard-hitter'.

'Come in, Mr Tovey, said Holmes. 'The hour is late and the weather is cold. Take a seat by the fire. This is my friend and colleague Dr Watson and you must tell us how we can help you.'

When Mr Tovey replied his manner was courteous but his voice was quiet and he spoke with a very pronounced Welsh accent.

'You are very kind, Sir,' he began, 'I will sit down, but I must not detain you for more than a moment or two. My errand, you see, is a trifling one and I am sorry to take up your time with it. In point of fact, I am a clerk with the National Vigilance Association and I have taken the liberty of calling on behalf of my mother, Mrs Tovey.

'My mother is a most respectable lady, Mr Holmes. For many years she was housekeeper to a clergyman in Cheltenham but she lives alone now and I am sorry to say she is not very well just at present. The fact is, her mind is going, poor soul, and she has begun to behave in a most eccentric fashion. I will not trouble you with a catalogue of her peculiar habits but one of them is to send small items of no particular consequence to distinguished persons. To mention just two examples, last month she sent the Archbishop of York a thimble. Then a few days ago – I tell you this with some embarrassment – she sent a mousetrap to a member of the Royal family. I am very much afraid, Mr Holmes, that she has now added you to her list of illustrious correspondents.

'May I ask,' he said, dropping his voice and speaking more quietly than ever, 'have you by any chance, in the last day or so, received through the post such a thing as a brass key?'

'I take it,' said Holmes, 'that unlike the mousetrap and the thimble the key is something you would wish to retrieve?'

'Well I would like to return it to her, yes indeed, for she had no business to part with it and its loss would cause some trifling inconvenience.'

'Alas, I cannot help you, Mr Tovey.'

'You have not received anything of the sort?'

'As I say, I cannot help you. However, if you would care to leave your card I shall be happy to send you a wire should anything further transpire.'

'Oh no, Mr Holmes, you must not put yourself to that trouble. There may be some mistake you see for the old lady can be very confused. Let me speak to her again and if she insists that she did indeed post the key I will send you a stamped addressed envelope. Then if the key should come to light you can simply put it in the envelope and drop it in the post to me.'

'By all means,' said Holmes and as our visitor had already risen from his seat stepped briskly across the room to open the door for him.

The whole interview had lasted no more than five minutes but as Holmes returned to his seat I noticed his lean features had a look of particular concentration and for a moment or two, with his eyes half closed, he seemed lost in thought. Then he looked up suddenly and said, 'There are times, Watson, when I regret that my profession as a consulting detective obliges me to work single-handed, although from time to time with your invaluable assistance. If we were at Scotland Yard I would have a plain-clothes officer on that man's tail as soon as he left the building and by midnight we should know who he is and where he lives. As it is, he has disappeared into the night along with five million other souls in this great metropolis. Still, should the need arise, it should not be difficult to trace a prosperous Chinese conjurer who gives a matinée performance at a London theatre on a Thursday afternoon.'

'My dear Holmes, you have quite lost me! Mr Tovey appears to be, as he says, a respectable clerk. Why on earth do you describe him as a Chinese conjurer?'

'You know my methods, Watson. Did you notice nothing about his personal appearance?'

'His voice is weak, but that I think is a long-standing condition for he appears to be in good health and his eyes are bright and clear. He wears spectacles but they are not of a very strong prescription.'

'Of no prescription at all for they are plain glasses – theatrical spectacles worn only to alter his appearance, impart an air of respectability and of course to disguise the fact that he is in the habit of shaving his eyebrows.'

'Why should any man do such a thing?'

'I suppose because he is often in greasepaint, in some guise where the bristling black eyebrows of a native Welshman would be distinctly out of place, so he chooses to improve on nature by wearing, or painting on, false eyebrows. Such were my suspicions when he first came into the room. They were confirmed when I took the trouble to show him to the door. The greasepaint, for the moment, has gone, but only within the last hour or so for he has removed it with cold cream and the aroma still lingers. Even so, I fancy I detected a small trace of Leichner's No. 8 below his left ear.'

'Well that explains why you think he is in the theatre but why do you put him down as a magician?'

'He is not on the legitimate stage for his voice would

hardly carry into the next room, let alone to the gallery of a theatre and no London manager would give him a speaking part. That leaves only the music halls and the minstrel shows. But since he is no singer he can only have what is known in the profession as a speciality. He is not an athlete, so he cannot be a strong man, contortionist or comic dancer. A Ventriloquist is equally out of the question. There are some animal acts – you will not have forgotten the terrible ordeal of Captain Blazer and his performing sea lions – but an animal act would hardly call for exotic make up. That leaves only the profession of conjurer for which, with his talent for deceit, I should think Mr Tovey admirably suited.'

'But why Chinese? And why prosperous?'

'Many conjurers are, or pretend to be, from India or the Far East: no doubt their flowing robes are helpful in some of their deceptions. But false or exaggerated eyebrows suggest an oriental rather than an Indian appearance and No. 8 is the greasepaint used for an oriental complexion. I have employed it myself for that purpose on one or two occasions. As to his prosperity, his clothes were well cut and his hand-made boots must have cost him two guineas at least. Always look at a man's boots, Watson. They will generally tell you all you need to know about the state of his household economy.'

'Well now that you explain the matter in that way, I see that our visitor may have been less than candid. I suppose that is why you told him you did not have they key?'

'I said only that I could not help him. He knows very well that I have the key.'

'How so?'

'Because at the very moment it was mentioned he saw you glance at the mantelpiece. My dear fellow, spare your blushes! It was a natural reaction and you must not blame yourself.'

'I had no reason to suppose he was deceiving us,' I replied, with some embarrassment. 'Indeed my thoughts were with his mother. Senile dementia can be a terrible affliction for the patient and her family.'

'I have no more belief in his mother's illness than I have in the mousetrap or the thimble or the National Vigilance Association.'

'But the envelope in which the key arrived was addressed in a very frail hand and Baker Street was spelt with two 'B's which certainly suggests some frailty of the mind.'

'The key and its envelope,' said Holmes, taking them down from the mantelpiece, 'came from an old gentleman in Clerkenwell who may be frail and is certainly blind but whose conduct is perfectly rational.'

'You have discovered who he is!'

'Not yet discovered, Watson, for I have deduced no more than I have told you. The district I take from the postmark on the envelope. The handwriting is certainly masculine, an old-fashioned commercial hand, learned when the man was young and sighted but now betraying, as you say, the frailty of age and perhaps some haste or agitation. The unusual choice of pencil, rather than ink, is surely sensible for a blind correspondent who cannot see whether his inkwell is full or his pen charged and who, if he uses ink, may blot the page without knowing. But the double 'B' is conclusive. He has written the number 221B and formed the first letter of Baker Street when he is momentarily distracted or interrupted. He returns to his work a moment later and cannot recall whether he has written two capital 'B's or only one. To make sure, he writes a third. Only a blind man could make such a mistake. This may also explain why he spells my name incurrectly. He has heard it spoken, no doubt, but has never seen it in writing.

'His conduct is rational because unlike a thimble or a mousetrap, a key is a valuable item which he has sent in a stout envelope, as a man of business might do, for safe keeping. Doubtless he wrote a covering letter but here again his blindness has deceived him and in his agitation he has folded up and enclosed with the key a blank sheet of paper. The letter itself presumably remained on his writing table and has evidently fallen into the wrong hands.'

'But the label on the key is written in ink.'

'And in a different hand, as I recall,' said Holmes scrutinising it with his lens under the gaslight. 'Yes, just as I thought – this is a more feminine hand and these words were written fifty years ago or more.'

'Good Heavens! Why do you say so?'

'The ink has etched, almost imperceptibly, into the paper. It is probably a compound of black gall and ferrous sulphate. Small stationers used to make up such inks for their customers but they were generally of poor quality and have fallen out of use since the blue-black inks were invented in the 1830s.'

'And what do you make of the words, 'Here we are again'?

'Several possibilities occur to me, but we must remember that our correspondent cannot read the label for himself and may hesitate to show it to anyone else. He may not know what is written on it.'

'I suppose so,' I said, 'but this only puts Mr Tovey in a more mysterious light. Perhaps we shall learn more if he does indeed send you a stamped addressed envelope?'

'I do not expect to receive one. That was a quick-witted suggestion which he made only because he did not have a card to leave. Mr Tovey, if that is indeed his name, is not to be trusted. I shall replace the key on the mantelpiece and we shall see if its magnetic qualities attract any further visitors.'

Since Holmes was not inclined to discuss the matter further, I let the subject drop, while reflecting that we still knew very little about the mysterious key and its anonymous sender. For my own satisfaction I looked into Kelly's Commercial Directory, but could find no reference to the National Vigilance Association.

*   *   *

Holmes's remark about further visitors soon proved correct but our next visitor was of quite a different character. The following evening, at about the same time Tovey had called, I heard a disturbance and raised voices in the hall below. Holmes was out, and I was thinking of stepping on to the landing to investigate the noise when I heard footsteps running up the stairs and a moment later the door of the room was flung open. On the threshold stood a woman in her thirties, flushed and agitated and, it seemed to me, a little unsteady on her feet.

'What is the meaning of this?' I asked, while signalling to Mrs Hudson, who was gallantly following behind, that there was no cause for alarm. In answer the woman stepped into the room and slammed the door behind her.

'Where is my father's key, Mr Sherlock Holmes?' she demanded. She had clearly been drinking, and although she was respectably dressed her sunken cheeks and bloodshot eyes told me she was no stranger to the bottle.

'I am not Mr Sherlock Holmes,' I replied, 'and I do not have your father's key.'

'Well you don't deceive me, Mr Detective. I know who you are, and I know you've the old man's key, and I mean to stay until I get it.'

'My name is Dr Watson, I am a friend and colleague of Mr Holmes, who is not here at present. What is the meaning of this intrusion? Who are you and what is your name?'

'I am Maria Fabrino, and I am the old man's daughter – as if you didn't know it.'

'I assure you I know nothing of the sort, but if you care to explain yourself I shall be happy to pass on a message to Mr Holmes.'

'Why you're just as bad as the old man and I dare say he put you up to it, the old skinflint! He keeps every penny under lock and key and sends you the key to cheat me out of it. I don't know how I endure it – he sits there on his marble throne with his beard down to his waist and his peacocks strutting on the lawn while I've not had a new bonnet on my head these twelve months and can hardly find three bob for a bottle of port wine.'

'I do not believe you are in need of port or any other strong liquor, and since you seem unwilling to give a rational account of yourself I must ask you to leave.'

'Oh you've not heard the last of this, I can tell you! One of these days I shall finish him off.'

'I advise you to do no such thing.'

At this the woman tossed her head, looked defiantly about her and muttered an oath. Then, without another word, she turned on her heel, flounced out of the room and clattered downstairs. I heard the front door slam and stepping across to the window saw her striding down Baker Street towards the West End.

When Holmes returned, an hour or so later, I gave him a full account of our visitor and everything she had said. He listened in silence, standing in front of the fire, his fingers clasped beneath his chin. When I had concluded he asked, 'She made no mention of the label on the key?'

'None.'

'You did not take her address?'

'I had no opportunity. The woman was here for no more than two or three minutes. She had obviously been drinking and was evidently talking nonsense.'

'Did you follow my advice and look at her boots, Watson?' asked Holmes, with his head on one side like an inquisitive jackdaw.

'I did indeed, Holmes,' I said, with some satisfaction.

'They were scuffed and dirty, but well-made and not in want of repair. For all her protestations I do not believe she is impoverished.'

'Capital! And now, Watson, are we to expect a third visitor? What do you make of it all?'

'Maria Fabrino's visit throws no light on the mystery,' I replied, 'for what she said was fantastic and may have been invented on the spur of the moment. She may even be mentally deranged. I surmise that she is a servant out of work, who has heard something of a key, believes it to be valuable, and hopes to steal it. Perhaps we should re-consider Mr Tovey's account. Could you be mistaken, Holmes, about the pencilled handwriting? If our corres-pondent is a woman Tovey's explanation for his visit is quite understandable. He did not tell us where his mother is living now and she may well be in Clerkenwell. He had no need to mention her blindness and may have chosen not to do so, because that would only add to his distress and embarrassment.'

'No, Watson, Tovey is a fake, and for all her faults Miss Fabrino appears to be a very truthful young woman.'

'But Holmes, the marble throne, her father's beard down to his waist, and the peacocks strutting on the lawn!'

'Mere details, Watson, for which there is doubtless some rational explanation. Consider the substance of what she says. She wants money for drink and she threat-ens violence if she does not get it. What could be more candid? She cannot be troubled to invent a lie, and has not the wit to do so. Even when you tell her who you are she chooses to disbelieve you, with the low cunning which is characteristic of the less intelligent members of her class. With Tovey the case is quite different. Every detail of his story is carefully contrived for the best effect. In his hands the blind old man at the mercy of his inebriated daughter becomes a respectable, if somewhat eccentric, old lady – a clergyman's housekeeper no less.

Then, in place of a woman addicted to drink, we have a dutiful son who works for a benevolent foundation and I myself have become an "illustrious correspondent" to be ranked with princes and archbishops. No, Watson, it is all humbug and I don't believe a word of it. But one thing is certain, the two of them are in it together and I mean to get to the bottom of this case. It is time to act!'

Two minutes later he had sent for Mrs Hudson's boy, given him instructions, and was waiting impatiently at the window for his return. We had not long to wait, for the lad soon scampered up the stairs clutching an armful of newspapers.

'Now Watson,' said Holmes, 'we shall begin with *The Era*, which is the best of the theatrical papers and I shall be greatly obliged for your assistance.'

'What am I to look for?'

'For Tovey the Chinese conjurer, under whatever name he performs. Let us divide the paper between us. There are scores of advertisements for artistes and theatres and somewhere in these pages we shall find our man.'

We divided the paper as he suggested. Holmes spread his pages on the floor and kneeling over them ran his eye rapidly up and down the columns of print with that fierce concentration which I had come to expect when he was following up a new line of enquiry.

I sat in my armchair, and began to read the pages he had handed me. I glanced at the reports of 'A theatrical divorce' and 'A terrible accident at a bullfight in Mexico' but soon moved on to the tight columns of small advertisements which made up the bulk of the paper. I then realised that the work was more troublesome than I had supposed.

'Holmes,' I sighed, after a few minutes, 'this is no easy task. Some of the artistes advertise their line of work; here, for example, is "Mr Colthard, the Respectable Knockabout" and "Little Figaro, the Mimical Droll" but most simply mention their names and engagements: "Mr Rupert de Vere, at the Alhambra, Leicester Square; Miss Adelaide Gunn, now disengaged, etc., etc." For all we know Mr de Vere might be a Chinese conjurer and Miss Gunn might be a conjurer's assistant. The advertisements are in no sort of order, and I can find no reference to Tovey. It is like looking for a needle in a haystack.'

'A very large haystack,' agreed Holmes. 'There are sixty-nine music halls in the Metropolis and hundreds of artistes, including some of the most noble, and some of the most contemptible, of our fellow creatures. We must persevere. It may take some time but we shall find him out, of that I am sure. Remember we are only looking for artistes who give a matinee performance.

We returned to our work, and a few minutes later my patience was rewarded when my eye caught the following item—

THE OTTOMAN SALOON, PICCADILLY
LONDON'S TEMPLE OF WHOLESOME AMUSEMENT
FOR FOUR WEEKS ONLY
THE HONOURABLE CHANG-FU
THE GREATEST NECROMANCER OF THE AGE
REFINED FUN AND PROFOUND MYSTERY
FULL SUPPORTING COMPANY
PERFORMANCES DAILY AT 3.00 AND 8.00

'Why Holmes!' I cried, crossing the room to show him the paper, 'I believe I have found our man – a Chinese conjurer almost on our doorstep whose next performance begins in less than half an hour. If we take a cab now we can be in our seats before the curtain rises.'

'Well done Watson! I'll wager this is Tovey and as always you are ready for adventure. It is a most endearing characteristic. But I fancy tomorrow's matinée may suit our purpose better. For the moment let us send for a light supper, and then smoke our pipes.'

It was with keen anticipation that I set out with Holmes the following afternoon. The weather was fine, and we walked down to the Ottoman Saloon, bought our tickets and took our seats in the front stalls, just behind the orchestra pit. The theatre was not large and as I looked about me I saw that the audience was, for the most part, respectable and well-behaved, many of them youngsters with their aunts and mamas.

The little orchestra soon took its place and struck up a lively overture, the curtain rose and in a moment the show was under way. A troupe of Chinese dancers whirled and swirled their colourful banners as they bounded across the stage to the music of cymbals and flutes. They were followed by a juggler and plate spinner, a pair of novelty musicians and a fire eater. Then, to the sound of drums and firecrackers, a great dragon with a fearsome mask and a dozen pairs of legs came dancing and swaying off the stage and through the auditorium while the little girls in the audience screamed with delight. In a cacophony of sound the dragon made its way back on to the stage, a huge gong sounded, the dragon gave a final leap and the curtain fell to a hearty round of applause. Then came an intermission, with some animated lantern slides, after which the orchestra returned, and the second half of the performance began.

Now the curtain rose for the first time on the Honourable Chang-Fu. For a moment I could hardly recognise the man, but as he walked slowly to the front of the stage and bowed to the audience I could see that this was indeed our mysterious visitor. A light olive complexion and high, exaggerated eyebrows could not disguise the build and manner of the little Welsh gentleman who had smiled and nodded in our sitting room just two days earlier. But now he had two assistants, handsome young men, dressed like himself in heavy and ornate robes, all three of them with pigtails and little round, embroidered hats.

There followed a performance which, from first to last, kept his young audience entranced. While the orchestra played quietly in the background huge bunches of flowers and cascades of scarves and ribbons were spirited out of thin air. A pair of white doves sprang to life in a puff of smoke from a tiny cabinet, and a pitcher which had been empty a moment earlier poured forth a gallon of wine. Never once did the conjurer speak. After each trick he simply smiled and bowed, folding his arms within his sleeves.

Soon an assistant carried on to the stage a lacquered table on which stood a bright translucent globe. The orchestra was silent now and only a single flute was heard as the conjurer raised his hands above the globe and it mysteriously lifted into the air. Then followed a sort of ballet, with the globe gently rising and falling, darting and hovering, now high, now low, and all under the invisible command of the conjurer's upraised hands. For fully three minutes the audience was hushed, until the magic globe finally descended onto its plinth once more, as light as a feather. As the little table was carried off the conjurer took his bow to another round of applause, in which I was not ashamed to join myself.

Then a gong sounded and the orchestra began to play again. A low, heavy table was carried in from the wings and following demurely, with little steps and downcast eyes, came an oriental maiden in a rich silk robe.

'Maria Fabrino?' asked Holmes, in a whisper.

'I am sure of it,' I replied, trying hard to reconcile the delicate creature who now stood before me with the disreputable, inebriated woman whose visit had so unsettled me the day before. As she stood meekly to one side an ornate wooden chest, with great brass handles, was carried forward by the two assistants and lifted onto the table. Then the chest was opened, tilted and displayed, and struck with a heavy stave to show that it was solid and strong. The young woman came forward, and her hands were tied behind her back with a silken rope. Then she stepped up onto the table and crouched down inside the chest, and the lid was closed.

There followed an elaborate pantomime. Two great straps and buckles were fastened and padlocked across the top of the chest, securing it to the table. A white Pekinese dog was led in with a silver collar and chain, jumped up, and with a little bark took his seat on top of the chest. Finally the two assistants passed a wide silk ribbon through the handles, and twice around the length of the chest, before retiring to opposite sides of the stage, each holding one end of the ribbon.

When all was ready Chang-Fu stepped forward, faced the audience, and raised his hand for silence. The music stopped and with all eyes upon him the conjurer silently drew a small revolver from the folds of his garment. With this, standing only a few feet to one side, he slowly took aim, at arm's length, at the great chest. A drum began to roll as we watched and waited, in rapt attention. The drum roll came to a crescendo and abruptly ceased.

A moment later three rapid shots rang out from the revolver. Then, with a clash of cymbals, the orchestra struck up again. The Pekinese jumped down from his perch and the assistants threw aside their ribbon and rushed forward to unbuckle the great straps. Within seconds the chest was flung open and tilted forward.

With a gasp we could see that it was empty. It had never been out of our sight and the young woman had disappeared before our eyes. Then the conjurer stepped forward, bowed deeply and with a broad gesture of his arm directed our attention to the proscenium box, in the dress circle. There was the young lady, who rose from her seat with a smile, bowed demurely and then quietly turned away and left the box to return once more to the stage.

This was the climax of the show. The young audience applauded heartily as the curtain rose and fell and the company took their final bows. Then, 'Follow me!' said Holmes, urgently.

Two minutes later we had made our way round to the back of the theatre and the doorkeeper, slipping my shilling into his pocket, was knocking on the conjurer's dressing room door.

'Do come in, gentlemen' said the conjurer, his voice as quiet and his accent as strong as before. 'I noticed you in the front stalls and was hoping you would honour me with a visit.'

The room was cluttered and untidy, festooned with garments and theatrical properties of all descriptions, many of which, I suppose, had been left by previous occupants. The walls were decorated with press notices and theatrical post cards and the whole room was diffused with a peculiar stale and slightly musty atmosphere. The conjurer was seated at his dressing table in front of the old cigar box which evidently contained his stage make up. He was still wearing his oriental costume but had removed his pigtail and greasepaint and with perfect composure was smoking a Turkish cigarette.

'I do hope you enjoyed our little entertainment?' he continued.

'We have come on business Mr Tovey, if that is your real name,' replied Holmes.

'It is indeed' he replied, with the utmost urbanity.

'And this, no doubt,' said Holmes dryly, looking about him, 'is the headquarters of the National Vigilance Association.'

'Ah, there you have me Mr Holmes! But you must excuse my little stratagem. I am an illusionist, you see. Deception has become my second nature. I was born in Cardigan, I spoke nothing but Welsh until I was twelve, and I have spent most of my working life in one disguise or another. I began, you know, as a black-face man, in the serio-comic line – "Uncle Joseph and his plantation melodies." But then I fell ill and my voice failed, so for a little while I was "Harry Hubble and his human xylophone." Then I laid out a little capital in a more profitable line of business and became "The Honourable Chang-Fu, the greatest necromancer of the age." And so now I earn my living without uttering a word.'

The thought seemed to amuse him and he chuckled quietly to himself.

'I understand,' said Holmes, with some impatience, 'that you have interested yourself in the affairs of Maria Fabrino?'

'Ah! My little Maria,' said Tovey. 'I think, Dr Watson, you may have met her already, but perhaps when she was not at her best?'

'Is she here?' asked Holmes.

'She will have left by now, Mr Holmes. Should you wish to speak to her I would recommend you to look into the saloon bar of the nearest public house, which is probably the King Edward in Vine Street.'

'She appears to have a fondness for strong drink,' I said.

'Alas, Doctor, it is not unusual in our profession. Indeed, it is often encouraged by the management. They like us to drink in the theatre bars you know. It is said to be good for business. But I am beyond that myself; tee-total, you know, quite teetotal,' saying which he contemplated his cigarette and relapsed into silence.

'I am interested in the lady,' said Holmes, 'on behalf of her father with whom, I fancy, she is not on the best of terms.'

'I fear not,' said Tovey. 'Indeed for some time now she has become somewhat tiresome on the question of her father and her supposed inheritance. She believes, I think, that he is a wealthy man, who has been less than generous towards her.'

'Is she in need of money?'

'She has no reason to be so. I pay her five pounds a week, which I regard as a liberal remuneration, and she is not slow to spend it.'

'You know, of course, that her father sent me a key?'

'Together with a covering letter, I believe.'

'The letter, as you well know, was purloined by his daughter. I wish to see it, if you please.'

Tovey hesitated for a moment, then took a small sheet of writing paper from the drawer of his dressing table.

Holmes took it from him, studied it for a moment, and then handed it to me. The paper was cheap and the frail, pencilled handwriting I immediately recognised as similar to that on our mysterious envelope.

'Have the goodness to read it to us, will you Watson,' said Holmes.

I did so, not without difficulty as in places the words had run into one another. It was addressed from Exmouth Market and read as follows—

Dear Mr Holmes,

Please help me, Sir. Every day now I am threatened and bullied by one who should be most dear to me. I cannot part with my small treasure, which is all I have left, for that would betray a trust. So I have locked my little chest and send you the key. Will you keep it safe for me, sir, until I decide what is to be done?

I remain, sir, your humble and patriotic servant,

Giuseppe Fabrino.

'That is the letter Maria Fabrino showed me, Mr Holmes. When she discovered it she was even more troublesome than before, and determined to recover the key, which I believe opens a strong box, or something of the sort. To tell you the truth, she was beside herself with anger. She told me she would strangle the old man, or have him put out of the way.

'You see how it is with Maria. When she is sober she is quiet enough but when she is in drink she can be very disagreeable.'

'Then why not discharge her?'

'Because I need her for the act. Between ourselves, she is not an intelligent woman, but she has never once been late for a performance or rehearsal, and she does the business to perfection, drunk or sober. I have no complaints there. Of course the chest escape can be learned by anyone in half an hour. But the floating globe you see, is another matter. I need a very skilful assistant for that; she stands on a ladder in the wings, holding the other end of the invisible thread and makes the globe behave in a most mysterious way. Many are the hours we have practised that illusion and she does it to perfection. No, I could not replace Maria in a hurry.

'It is because I need to keep her that I persuaded her to leave the matter in my hands for a few days and agreed to practice my little deception on Dr Watson and yourself. I must confess I enjoyed the opportunity of a speaking part in the little drama I had written for myself. I decided that the aged parent should be a lady rather than a gentleman and I added one or two details for a better effect. I thought I had carried it off rather well, but you evidently saw through my disguise.'

'You seem to think,' I said, 'that helping a grasping young woman to get hold of her father's money was a matter for amusement. In my view it was the action of a scoundrel.'

'You may say so, Dr Watson. But you see, if I had not intervened she would have bullied him just as before, and probably worse. If I could retrieve the key without any unpleasantness, that would be something, would it not?

So I told her to leave everything to me and took it upon myself to pay you a visit. When I told her, the following day, that you had the key but declined to hand it over, she was beside herself and went off in a rage to meet Dr Watson. The rest you know.

'I am sorry your time has been taken up with this business, gentlemen and I regret now that I ever concerned myself in it. But you may rest assured that I shall wash my hands of it now and leave the old gentleman to make peace with his daughter.'

'I am afraid that is out of the question,' said Holmes. 'I now consider myself retained by Miss Fabrino's father who has asked for my help and protection. I intend to call on him within the hour and you, Sir, will have the goodness to accompany us.'

'I should like to help you, Mr Holmes, of course but on this occasion I must beg you to excuse me. The time draws on and I have another performance at eight this evening.'

'It is not yet six and you are not required until the second half of this evening's performance. There is time enough for our errand, which will take no more than an hour.'

'Alas, I cannot help you Mr Holmes.'

'I think you will find that it is in your best interests to co-operate with our investigation. I understand your company moves to the Bradford Temperance Halls in the new year. It would be most unfortunate if the Evening Telegraph were to expose the secret of your great illusion on the eve of your first performance.'

'Are you confident that you have discovered my professional secrets, Mr Holmes?'

'The trick is perfectly obvious to any scientific observer who is not distracted by your oriental mumbo-jumbo. Le Bouquet was working an identical illusion in Paris earlier this year and has now, I believe, moved to Berlin where he continues to deceive a gullible public.'

'You are remarkably well-informed about these matters. May I take it that if I undertake to help you this evening my professional secrets will be safe in your hands?'

'Certainly.'

'Very well then,' said the Welshman, with perfect affability. 'If you will give me time to change we will make all speed and pay our respects to Mr Fabrino.'

A few minutes later we were rattling north in a four-wheeler through the darkening streets of Clerkenwell and into the heart of Little Italy. In a short while we came to a halt in the narrow street known as Exmouth Market which, for all its bustle and excitement in the early morning, at this time of the evening was almost deserted, the silence broken only by the muffled sound of a piano and the buzz of conversation from a brightly lit public house on the corner.

We had pulled up outside a small terraced house, next to a second-hand book shop. Our knock at the front door was answered by a taciturn woman, plump and middle-aged, who soon disappeared down a dark passage. We caught a snatch of conversation, and after a minute or two the woman reappeared and with a nod took us through to a back room on the ground floor.

It was a remarkable sight that met our eyes as we stepped into the room. It was not large, and was lit by a single gas lamp which the woman had evidently just lighted. But as I looked about me I had the sensation of stepping into an oil painting of an Elysian landscape. The whole room, walls and ceiling alike, was painted up like a theatrical backdrop. In each corner was a pair of marble pillars. On the ceiling, painted doves nestled in alabaster alcoves, beneath a brilliant sky. Around the four walls ran a marble balustrade broken only, incongruously, by the domestic grate and the curtained window. Beyond the balustrade, on the wall opposite the fireplace, a green lawn sloped down to an ornamental lake with a distant prospect of ancient ruins standing in a great forest. A herd of deer grazed by the lake and, just as the man's daughter had described it, a pair of peacocks strutted on the lawn.

Seated at the head of this extraordinary room was the man we had come to see. Mr Fabrino was wearing a dressing gown and carpet slippers, with a red nightcap on his head. His beard, if it did not reach quite to his waist, was certainly very long, and he had a habit of fingering it, nervously. His eyes were sightless, although he turned his head towards us as we entered the room. I was instantly reminded of King Lear in his madness, and saddened to see the unmistakable signs of a recent contusion below the left eye.

His chair was no less remarkable than the rest of the room. It was tall and made of wood, but painted up in the semblance of a Roman throne, with marble masonry and elaborate carving. The other furniture in the room comprised two or three chairs and a side table, all of which were painted up in the Roman style and seemed to have been rescued from some theatrical warehouse. Beside him was a small table, on which stood a cup of cocoa and a biscuit.

As the door closed behind us the man spoke in a high-pitched voice which was yet clear and firm.

'Who is it?' he asked. 'Who's there?

'I am Sherlock Holmes, Mr Fabrino. With me is my colleague Dr Watson, and Mr Tovey, your daughter's employer.'

'Ah, Mr Holmes. How good of you to come, Sir. I had quite given up hope of hearing from you when my letter was stolen. But why is Mr Tovey with you? Has he come to take my daughter's part?'

'Not at all, sir,' said Tovey. 'I am here only because I may be able to exercise some influence over her.'

'I am very glad to hear it,' said Fabrino. 'Pray take a seat gentlemen. You are very quiet, Dr Watson. I suppose you are looking about you, at my room.'

'It is quite remarkable,' I said. 'I have seen nothing like it outside the theatre.'

'It is all my own work, Doctor. I spent my working life in the theatre, painting backdrops and side wings and the like. I was the first and the most rapid of all the men at Drury Lane and the Haymarket. This whole room took me no more than three days. I painted it when I first moved in here, ten long years ago. My sight was fading then and within six months it had gone, and I have hardly stirred from the room since.'

'I have your key,' said Holmes 'and Mr Tovey has shown me your letter. Do I understand you have something of value which you wish to secure from your daughter?'.

'It is all I have left now, Mr Holmes, for she has had so much over the years – all except my last little treasures, from which I shall never be parted on any account. I tell her they are worthless but she will not believe me. They were given to me by a better woman than she, a kind and sober woman, and I have them on trust and cannot let them fall into her hands.'

'If I am to help you, you must tell me what these treasures are.'

'I will show you,' said Fabrino, saying which he reached into a recess at the base of his Roman chair and took out a small casket, like a miniature sea chest, with brass corners and brass handles at either end. This he carefully placed on the table beside him, but for the moment made no attempt to open. Instead he paused and appeared to look round the room with his sightless eyes. His head was tilted to one side and his fingers were nervously running through his beard.

At length, 'You have heard tell of Mr Grimaldi?' he asked.

'Why, who has not!' said Tovey. 'Joe Grimaldi was the greatest pantomime, the greatest clown, that ever was. His name is a legend in the profession. Very old fashioned now, I dare say, but in his time quite a legend!'

'I knew Grimaldi,' said the old man. 'I saw him at Sadlers Wells a dozen times or more when I was a lad. He lived just two doors away in this very street, at Number 56, over the ironmongers.

He was a great favourite with us boys, especially. Many a time have I seen him leap on to the stage with his little bow legs and his clown's face crying "Here we are again! Here we are again!" Then how we laughed, for we knew we were in for some fun. Oh the tricks he played! Leaping in and out of shopfronts, stealing sausages and guzzling food. I have seen him run out of the wings with two ducks in one pocket and a little piglet in the other, all alive and kicking. Then, when we screamed with delight, he would pull a long face and say, "For shame! For shame!"

'And such invention! I have seen that man turn a couple of beer barrels and a basket of vegetables into a pair of marching soldiers in less time than it takes to tell it. How we looked forward to those pantomimes and the old cry – "Here we are again!"

The old man smiled at the recollection, and then continued.

'Now the reason I saw Grimaldi so often was, my own family was in the theatrical business and as a young boy I was quite a favourite behind the scenes at one or two of the London theatres.

'Well I am sorry to say, Joe Grimaldi grew old before his time. The business knocked him about so, you see, that eventually he had to turn it in. I was there, at Drury Lane, as a lad, almost sixty years ago, on the night of his farewell performance. I was only twelve years old but I could see Joe was just a shadow of his former self. He had not performed for some time and now he was thin and old, and the sparkle had gone out of his eyes.

'He could tumble no longer and had to perform in his clown's dress, sitting down. He did the barber shop scene from *The Magic Fire* and sang *Hot Codlins* and made a little speech. He was on stage for no more than half an hour and I do believe that was the last time he set foot in a theatre.

'Now one of the party behind the scenes was Miss Fanny Kelly. She was the lovely Columbine who had played in *Harlequin Quicksilver*, earlier in the evening and she had such a foolish, whimsical idea. She told me that the ancient Romans, at the funeral of a loved one, would collect their tears in a glass bottle to preserve them for evermore. Well Miss Fanny's idea was that Joe Grimaldi's last performance would bring tears of laughter and affection, and all her theatrical friends in the wings should shed a tear into her little perfume bottle, which she would then present to Joe at the end of the performance.

'Alas, there were tears enough, but tears of sadness, not laughter, for truth to tell, Joe was a broken man, and a broken-hearted one. Miss Fanny wept a little herself, as did two or three of the other young dancers, and one or two of the men, who could remember happier times. In the end she had not the heart to give her little present to Joe. Instead she labelled it in her neat hand, with his old catch line, and put it away in this little casket of hers for safe keeping.

'I soon went into the theatre myself, but in the scenery business, for I was never a performer, and as the years went by I collected one or two relics of Grimaldi.

'Many years later I met Miss Fanny, now a widow, and she remembered me as her little Fabrino. We recalled that night at Drury Lane and she said I must have been one of the youngest in the theatre. We spoke of how Joe's son, Grimaldi junior, had gone to the bad. I told her of the few things I had collected over the years, and how I had moved into this house, just two doors down from Joe's old home. The upshot was, she entrusted her little casket to me, to which I added the few curios I had already collected. And now if you will hand me the key I shall show you my treasure.'

Holmes did so, and he opened the casket.

'Now I cannot see these things myself, and it is many a year since I looked on them, so you must take them out yourselves and tell me what you find.'

'What have we got, Watson?' asked Holmes.

'Here are some newspaper cuttings,' I said, 'with an account of the last performance and some old letters, perhaps from artistes who remembered Grimaldi. Here is a portrait of him, a theatrical print, with tinsel and spangles; some old penny plain and tuppenny coloured scenes, with some figures, Harlequin, Columbine and Clown. Here is some sheet music, and here a pot of white paint for the face, a pot of rouge and some theatrical pencils.

'And this,' I said, taking out a small item carefully wrapped in a silk handkerchief, must be the vial of which you spoke.'

'Why yes!' broke in Tovey 'and here are the very tears the pretty girl shed all those years ago, still preserved in this little glass bottle as bright and fresh as they day they stole down her cheek.' As he said this he silently winked at Holmes and myself, for we could both see that the vial was crusted and empty, the contents long since evaporated.

'I was fearful of losing it,' said Fabrino. 'I knew Joe Grimaldi's son took to drink and I could see my own daughter going the same way. These things mean nothing to her. She thinks I am a rich man, but I have nothing. She would sell anything for drink, even my little relics, if she had half a chance, but I want them kept safe, for I must now be one of the last who ever saw the great clown perform.

'She was here last week, you know. She says she comes from affection, but I know better. She comes for money and anything else she can lay her hands on. She wanted me to give her my casket for safe keeping but I knew it would have been in hock to the pawnbroker within the hour. We quarrelled and she marched out, slamming the door behind her as she always does when she is in one of her fits.

'When she left I was in such a state of agitation I wrote to you at once. I can still write, you see, I have not lost that facility. I had heard of you, Mr Holmes, and knew no one else to turn to, for all my old theatrical friends have passed on. I could not send you the casket but I did send you the key and asked my landlady to post the letter for me. But I was in such distress, as you know now, that I must have knocked the letter on the floor and sent you a blank piece of paper, for I am sure I did put a sheet of writing paper in the envelope.

'Next day, my daughter came round again, to make amends, or so she said. Then she saw the letter on the floor under my table, and read it. "Why," she says "You rotten old miser, you skinflint! You've sent it away." Then she hit me – my own daughter, Mr Holmes! She struck me across the face, may God forgive her, for I am sure I have done her no wrong.

'Well, it has all come out now. Who knows what she will say or do when she learns that you have been here, gentlemen. I fear for my safety, indeed I do.'

'At least you need not fear for your treasure,' said I. 'Mr Holmes, I know, will be willing to keep it safe for you, if you care to entrust it to him.'

'I rather think that is your department, Watson,' said Holmes. 'You are the keeper of our archives and admirably methodical in that line of work. Mr Fabrino, would you be content for Dr Watson to have the care of your casket and its contents?'

'By all means,' the old man replied. 'You would do me a great kindness, Doctor, to keep it safe, and quite beyond her reach.'

'I shall be happy to do so,' I replied. 'You can depend on me for that. But I too am alarmed for your safety. Is there nothing that will restrain your daughter?'

'The law will restrain her,' said Holmes, 'in the person of my friend and colleague Inspector Hopkins of Scotland Yard, who is unhappily familiar with cases of this sort. Mr Tovey, you tell me Miss Fabrino has one virtue at least, that she is always prompt. I shall want to see her in your room at the theatre on Monday evening, precisely one hour before the performance begins.'

'I am sure that can be arranged,' said Tovey.

'Very well. Then we shall take our leave. Mr Fabrino, I wish you well. Your treasure is now in safe hands, and I have reason to believe that your daughter will not be disposed to ill treat you again.'

The old man thanked us profusely, without rising from his chair, and we went out into the cold night air, the precious casket under my arm.

* * *

I was not present at the theatre the Monday evening, but when Holmes returned I asked him how the interview had gone.

'Hopkins was good enough to accompany me. I reminded Miss Fabrino that she was growing older, and that since she was a notorious drinker her future employment now rested only on her reputation for punctuality. Hopkins told her that he has a constable on patrol in Exmouth Market who will take particular care to look in on her father from time to time, and that if there was the slightest harm to the old man she would be arrested at the theatre, before the evening performance. Should that happen, in all likelihood, she would never work again.'

'And do you suppose she will heed the warning?'

'We can only hope so, Watson. I fancy she has seen the inside of a police cell once or twice before and will not wish to repeat the experience. Besides, she knows now that her father has nothing in his room of any value to her.'

'So she will continue to delight little children and their mamas, who know nothing of her true character, by her miraculous escape from the great Chinese chest. Tell me Holmes, how is that managed? The revolver, of course, was firing blanks for I saw no recoil, but as to the rest, I confess I am quite baffled by the illusion.'

'As I told Tovey, the trick is perfectly obvious to a scientific observer. The heavy lid of the chest, the straps and padlocks, and the silken ribbon, are all designed to make us believe that the chest cannot be opened in the regular way, and the girl cannot burst out of it. But none of those elaborate precautions prevent a panel at the rear of the chest from opening inward, when a secret catch is released. That done, it is the work of a moment for the girl to scramble out, push the silk ribbon to one side, replace the panel, and conceal herself behind the table until the curtain falls.'

'But there was nowhere to hide. The table had four stout legs and we could see beneath it.'

'So you could, at first, but recollect that you were never shown the rear of the table. From there, no doubt when your attention was distracted by the Pekinese, a small curtain was released, identical to the dark backcloth at the rear of the stage. From that moment, although you could still see the legs of the table, and fancied you could still see beneath and beyond it, your line of vision was in fact obstructed and the area just behind the table was concealed from view.'

'The girl's wrists were tied.'

'With a slip knot, which would not delay her for more than a moment or two.'

'But somehow she must make her way, in just a few seconds, to the box in the dress circle.'

'That would be impossible, and is also unnecessary. The woman in the box was fully two inches taller than the woman on the stage. She is a double, one of the dragon dancers no doubt, dressed in identical clothes and made up to a very similar appearance. She is only in sight for two or three seconds, just long enough to take a bow and depart. The two women are not identical, but they are never seen together and the audience will naturally assume that they are one and the same.'

'Why how very obvious! Elementary, in fact.'

'As I have often remarked, Watson, there is no difficulty in understanding any mystery when once it has been carefully explained. Men like Tovey earn their living only because the public wishes to be mystified and will pay handsomely for the privilege of being deceived.'

'Come Holmes,' I said, 'You are not above such things yourself and have more than once taken satisfaction in a *coup de théâtre* at the conclusion of your own investigations.'

To this remark Holmes made no reply but I fancy a thin smile crossed his lips as he reached for the Persian slipper and the black shag tobacco.

THE NORFOLK BARONET

FROM time to time, especially in the long winter evenings after the death of my poor wife, when time seemed to hang heavily on my hands, I would rouse myself, take a brisk walk round to Baker Street, and call in on my friend Sherlock Holmes. It was good to see the old rooms we used to share together and Holmes was always ready with a warm welcome and a glass of brandy. We would sit on either side of the fire, smoking our pipes and recalling some of the many cases in which we had collaborated over the years; some tragic and horrible, some memorable for the remarkable chain of reasoning with which Holmes had exposed the truth, and a few which we remembered only with affection and amusement. One such, which never failed to bring a smile to my friend's lips, I am now at liberty, after the passage of some years, to place before the public.

Our adventure had begun on a bright July morning with the light streaming in through the windows of our sitting room while we lingered over breakfast, reading the newspapers. After a while Holmes, who was in a languid mood, put down his paper and turned his attention to the morning post.

'Now here Watson,' he said, 'is an item of great rarity and value,' flourishing the first letter he opened, and holding it up for my inspection.

'That is the crest of the Diogenes Club – a letter from your brother Mycroft, no doubt.'

'Precisely so, for it is indeed a rare occurrence when Mycroft exerts himself sufficiently to lift pen to paper. Let us see what he has to say.'

My dear Sherlock,

I should be greatly obliged if you could see your way to helping my young friend Cheffington, who is disappointed that a noble baronet did not invite him to lunch and is troubled about an overdue library book. He will call tomorrow at ten, if convenient.

Regards, Mycroft

Then at the very foot of the letter Mycroft had written—

$$q + v = ?$$

'What an extraordinary request! Is your brother in earnest, or is this some kind of practical joke? And what is the meaning of this cryptic equation?'

'I am sure he is in earnest, for I have never known him to engage in any sort of prank. Indeed, I suspect this is something more serious than his facetious letter would suggest. As to the equation, I can only suppose he is pointing out some aspect of the case which has caught his attention. But who is Mr Cheffington? The name is unusual, and I fancy I have come across it before. Would you be good enough to glance in my index Watson, and see if he merits an entry?'

I took down one of the bulging ledgers in which, from time to time, Holmes pasted, in some sort of alphabetical order, any items of interest which happened to catch his eye. His index, as he called it, was in fact an encyclopaedic catalogue of crime and the criminal underworld, chemical and scientific papers, bizarre and inexplicable events, and a quantity of other information, some clipped from the daily papers, and some written in his own remarkably neat and rapid hand. Passing over entries for Chen Hau Yan of the Ever Victorious Army, Charcoal (its combustible properties) and Charmaine Delavine, the American adventuress, I came upon the entry I was looking for.

'Here it is Holmes: *Rupert Lemuel Henry Cheffington, born 1862, educated at Eton and Oriel College, Oxford, called to the Bar 1884, and shortly afterwards appointed Bluemantle Pursuivant of Arms.* And what, pray, is a Pursuivant of Arms?'

'We are in exalted company, Watson. He is one of the heralds at the College of Arms where they study the old records, grant new coats of Arms, and proclaim the accession of the new sovereign – a duty for which they have not been summoned, Dear Boy, since many years before you and I were born. Mycroft wrote yesterday, so our client will be here within the hour. I trust you are free, for the case promises to be something out of the ordinary.'

Within the hour Mr Cheffington was shown up to our room. I had expected a herald to evoke something of the pomp and pageantry of medieval tournaments but our visitor proved to be a rather studious man in his early thirties, slightly built and soberly dressed. He blinked at us above his wire-framed spectacles and his face looked tense and drawn.

'Mr Cheffington,' said Holmes, 'pray take a seat. Dr Watson and I have been reading my brother's letter of introduction. Let me show you what he says.' With a twinkle in his eye Holmes handed over Mycroft's note, which Cheffington read without a smile, pursing his lips.

'I am afraid this letter makes light of the matter, Mr Holmes,' he said, 'and I simply do not understand the cryptic marks at the end. However, I must tell you that this case has caused me the greatest anxiety. The library book to which your brother refers is a precious heirloom and its loss is sufficiently serious that I am authorised to incur whatever expenditure may be necessary, without limit, to recover it.'

'Pray continue,' said Holmes. I assure you that we shall treat the matter no less seriously than you do yourself.'

'Thank you,' said Cheffington. 'I must tell you, Mr Holmes, that the library of the College of Arms is unique. It contains hundreds of volumes, chiefly rolls of arms and other learned works, some of them dating back many centuries. The earlier volumes are all hand-written, of course, generally on parchment, and lavishly illustrated with shields of arms, heraldic beasts and ancient pedigrees. There is nothing to equal the collection in the whole of Europe and I need hardly say it has been most carefully catalogued and preserved through the ages.'

Holmes listened intently, his eyes closed, his fingertips touching and his head a little on one side.

'In one episode in our history,' our visitor continued, 'we take particular pride. In the great fire of London, in

1666, as the wind drove the flames westward from the City, the College and its library were threatened with destruction. But the heralds and their servants were equal to the occasion. Every single volume was carried away by water and lodged safely at Whitehall. The College was burned, but the books were safe and in due course, when the College was rebuilt, the books were returned.

'Now each year, on the second Sunday in September a short ceremony is held in the great court, in the presence of a few distinguished guests. The Earl Marshal presides, and we – that is the heralds and pursuivants – present ourselves at the bar of the Court in our tabards. The Earl Marshal asks Richmond Herald, "Are all the ancient rolls and books entrusted to our care now well secured within the precincts of this Honourable Court?"

'To which Richmond replies, "All safe My Lord, and all secure."

"And so do you all affirm, upon your honour?" asks the Earl Marshal, whereupon we all make a deep bow, by way of assent and the chaplain intones, "Thanks be to God for this deliverance." The court then adjourns, and we join our guests for sherry and biscuits in an anteroom.

'Perhaps you will smile at our little ceremony, gentlemen, but I could not make my bow to the Earl Marshal, upon my honour, if I knew that a book in my charge had gone astray. In such a case I should feel obliged to resign my place.'

'And evidently that is what you now fear,' said Holmes. 'Pray continue.'

'I have a friend, a baronet, Sir Archie Hanneford. We

were at Oxford together and share a common interest in antiquities. He inherited his title from his father some years ago. It is a Norfolk family, not wealthy, I believe, but well-respected in the county and the title is an old one for Hanneford is the tenth baronet.

'In the past he has spent much of his time in London, but about a year ago his mother died and he took over the family seat at Castle Acre. It is called Hanneford Hall but is really no more than a large house on the River Nar.

'Four weeks ago, to the day, I had business in Norfolk and decided to call in on Hanneford. In all courtesy I should have dropped him a line beforehand, but my decision was made on the spur of the moment and I felt sure he would welcome a visit from an old friend.

'I took the branch line from Thetford and soon found the house which is only a short walk from the station. I arrived shortly after noon and my knock was answered by Hanneford himself. To my surprise, for in London he was always clean-shaven and had excellent eyesight, he had grown a beard and was wearing an eyeglass.'

'Does he incline to foppery?' asked Holmes.

'On the contrary, he is generally rather careless of his personal appearance. But it was not his appearance which unsettled me so much as his behaviour. We have always been on excellent terms but on this occasion his greeting was somewhat reserved and he seemed ill at ease, almost apprehensive.

'However, he invited me in and we enjoyed a few minutes awkward conversation in his sitting room. To tell the truth I thought he might offer to show me the house and gardens, and I almost hinted as much, but he seemed disinclined to do so. After a while, however, he seemed a little more relaxed and suggested I stay for a bite of lunch.

'Then there was a knock on the door and his housekeeper entered. I knew her at once. Her name is Jennifer Price and she used to look after Hanneford when he lived in London. In fact I have known her almost as long as I have known him. She is what used to be called a "good creature" and I believe she is a very competent housekeeper. If she has a fault, however, it is that she can be a little over-familiar. In short, she is inclined to gossip, and a few minutes in her company can seem a long time.

'Seeing me in the room she smiled and said "Good afternoon, Sir." I replied, "Good afternoon, Jennifer. As you see, I have come to visit, and I have been invited to stay for lunch."

'Well I am very pleased to hear it, Sir," she said, "and we must have a nice talk before you go. You can tell me all what's happening in Town and I must show you my beehives, for I keep bees now we live in the country."

'At the mention of beehives Hanneford's manner seemed to change.

"No, no," he said, 'I am afraid, on second thoughts, lunch is quite out of the question. In fact, I have just recollected that I am expecting another visitor this afternoon. Besides, the train is not always reliable. I think if you leave now, Cheffington, you will be in time for the two o'clock connection, but you must make haste, make haste!"

'All this was said in such an agitated, excitable way that I was positively embarrassed, so I picked up my hat and stick and took my leave. Hanneford saw me to the door, we shook hands and I walked down the front garden path. As I did so I noticed Mrs Price had made her way to a side door, from where she was discreetly signalling to me. Thinking she might have something to impart, I walked just a short distance up the street and then waited for a minute or two out of sight of the house.

'I had not long to wait before she appeared, in a state of some agitation. "Oh I am sorry you are sent away like this, Sir," she said. "I declare, it's too bad of him, just because he doesn't like my poor bees."

'"But he has another visitor," I protested, "and I really should have written before calling."

'"Begging your pardon, Sir," she said, "there ain't no other visitor, I know that, for sure, and the next train's not for an hour or more. That's just his way of getting rid of you. But he has been very peculiar since we moved down here. I'm not sure he's right in the head, sometimes. It runs in the family if you ask me. I believe his poor father was took very similar at the end."

'I had no wish to prolong this conversation, so I made some non-committal remark and turned to continue on my journey. Then I heard a shout; "Make haste, Cheffington, make haste!" Hanneford was standing in the street outside his house and positively shooing me away. I set off at once, but looking back, I noticed that he stood there watching me until I was four or five hundred yards off, as if to make quite sure that I would not retrace my steps.

'On the journey home I had time to think about what Mrs Price had said. It was the estrangement of an old friend, and the hint of insanity in the family which most concerned me but of course I was quite powerless to help in such a delicate case.

'The following day, at the College, a thought struck me. One of the books in the library was a history and pedigree of Hanneford's family. It was first written, in longhand, in the 17th century and had been added to, from time to time, by successive members of the family. Hanneford himself had sometimes perused the volume and I believe his late father had added some details of the more recent family history himself. It occurred to me that if there was any history of insanity in the family there might be some reference to it in this book. I went down to the library at once, to consult it. To my dismay, it was missing from its place on the shelves. I searched for an hour or more, but without success. The book was nowhere to be found and inevitably my suspicions fell on my old friend.'

'Had he ever been permitted to borrow the book?' I asked.

'Certainly not. That would have been quite out of the question, for this was one of the precious books which had been rescued from the great fire. Indeed he was only allowed to use the library on my personal introduction, some years ago, which is why I hold myself responsible for his good behaviour.

'I wrote to Hanneford within the hour; a tactful letter,

simply asking if he knew anything of the book's whereabouts. I had no reply to that, nor to the letters which I wrote in the two following weeks. I became seriously alarmed, for we are nearing the end of July and the annual ceremony is only six weeks hence.

'You can imagine it was with some trepidation that I eventually confided in my colleague, Richmond Herald, for I had been hoping to deal with the matter privately. Richmond was deeply concerned and has undertaken to meet the cost of any enquiries. He is a member of the Diogenes Club and it was he who suggested I should speak to Mr Mycroft Holmes. I did so, and he referred me to Dr Watson and yourself.'

'Describe the book, if you please,' said Holmes.

'It is a slim folio, bound in vellum, with the title endorsed on the spine in pen and ink. Even to the casual glance it is obviously a book of some antiquity, but it is otherwise unremarkable in outward appearance.'

'Could Hanneford have taken it out of the library without being seen?'

'It is not impossible. A librarian is always on duty but if his attention was distracted for a moment or two the book could have been concealed.

'Mr Holmes,' he continued, 'I entreat you to help me. My whole professional life has been spent in the College of Arms and to resign in disgrace would be a terrible blow.'

'There is no disgrace if you are not to blame,' said Holmes. 'However the case is not without interest and I shall be happy to undertake some enquiries on your behalf. Will you leave it with me for a day or so, while I consider how best to proceed?'

'Of course,' said Cheffington, and with many expressions of gratitude took his leave.

'Insanity is more in your line than mine, Doctor,' said Holmes, when our visitor had left. 'Do you see any evidence of it here?'

'Eccentricity, perhaps,' I replied. 'Insanity is probably too strong a word. Besides, it seems to me there may be a perfectly simple explanation for the man's behaviour.'

'I should be glad to hear it,' said Holmes.

'Why, there may be some irregularity in Hanneford's domestic arrangements with the housekeeper; something which he feared might come to light if Cheffington's visit was prolonged.'

'But that would not account for his purloining the book, or his failure to reply to Cheffington's letters. No, Watson, there are some things, innocuous in themselves, which taken together assume a fresh significance. The noble baronet sports an eyeglass and grows a beard. He alters his appearance, conceals his family history and is at pains to curtail his housekeeper's gossip. The man has something to hide, and when we know what it is we shall have got to the bottom of this little mystery. I am fully engaged for the next day or two but after that, what do you say to a little coarse fishing on the River Nar?'

'A capital suggestion,' I said. 'I will have a word with McAlister and ask him to look after my practice while I am away.'

So it was that at the end of the week we found ourselves on the Great Eastern Railway, rattling across the Cambridgeshire fens towards the ancient forest of Thetford. It was late afternoon when we pulled into the station at Castle Acre, and were able to look about us. We found a sleepy village, with cottages and outbuildings clustered along a broad, single street, below which the ground fell away towards the river and the ruins of the great Norman Priory. The porter recommended a local inn where we soon found good accommodation and a hearty meal.

Later in the evening we strolled to the outskirts of the village and found Hanneford Hall. It was an impressive Georgian house, set well back from the road, with a long garden running down to the river, much as Cheffington had described it. The lights were not yet lit, and there were no signs of occupation, so, for the time being, we continued on our way.

The following morning, after breakfast, we parted company. Holmes strolled into the village while I walked down to the river and found a pleasant spot beneath an overhanging oak. There I spent a few hours in the warm sunshine accounting for half a dozen roach and a ferocious little perch, who struggled on the line for two or three minutes. For company I had only the black cattle grazing on the water meadows below the priory and a wily heron on the opposite bank who, in the hour or so he stood there, proved to be a more successful angler than myself.

*　　*　　*

'I have made a good beginning,' said Holmes, as we sat

down to dinner that evening. 'I called at the back of the house and found Mrs Price very willing to show her bees to an enthusiastic metropolitan visitor such as myself. She has three hives and is remarkably knowledgeable on the segregation of the queen. Moreover, just as Cheffington said, she is a fund of gossip. From her I learned more about the village in an hour than I would have learned from my Baedeker in a fortnight.'

'Were you not interrupted?'

'No. Hanneford never goes near the hives and kept to his rooms as I believe he generally does after his early morning walk. I left before noon and promised to return tomorrow with a copy of *Langstroth*. It is the beekeeper's bible, I believe. I took the precaution of buying a good second-hand copy before we left London.

'By the by, Watson,' he continued, "there is a young lad in the village who would like to meet you. He lives with his mother who is a Hindu, or a Sikh. She is said to be a soldier's widow, and the lad looks to enlist as a drummer boy. I took the liberty of suggesting that he would find you near the bridge tomorrow afternoon and that you would have much to tell him about life in the Army.'

'I shall be delighted to help, if I can. But does this have any bearing on our enquiries?'

'I hope that it might, and as the boy will be plying you with questions I hope he, in turn, can be persuaded to tell you something about himself and his mother. She, I fancy, is a woman of strong character.'

The following afternoon, obedient to Holmes's wishes, I took up my rod at the riverside. I had not long to wait before the lad appeared. He was a good looking half-caste, about sixteen years old. Tall and slender, with delicate features and remarkably bright blue eyes, he carried himself well, and gave every appearance of a smart young man.

He told me his name was Sam Bristow, and that Sam was short for Samrath, meaning 'mighty and powerful'. He did indeed want to join the Army as a musician. It appeared that Mrs Price had spoken to his mother, recommending that he in turn should speak to the "military gentleman" (for so I was described) who was staying at the inn.

I told the lad of my time as a surgeon in the Berkshires, and something of what I knew about a bandsman's life; of the dozens of bugle calls he would have to learn, of how, on campaign, the bandsmen played behind the lines to keep up the spirits of the fighting men and in battle went forward as stretcher bearers to rescue the wounded.

The lad listened with a keen interest, asking numerous questions, but all in a most respectful way. Mindful of what Holmes had said, I questioned him in turn, to discover what I could of his family.

He told me his father had been an officer in the Bengal Lancers, with a scarlet tunic and a blue turban. He said he had died when rescuing a wounded comrade on the North-West frontier. His widowed mother, he told me, was an Indian princess. She had brought him to England as a baby, but one day he would claim his inheritance, for his father had been the son of a great nobleman, enlisted under an assumed name.

All this romancing I took with a pinch of salt, but the lad was so much in earnest and spoke so well of his parents that I hesitated to advance any comment, and contented myself with listening to his story.

After we had been talking for about twenty minutes Holmes appeared, unexpectedly, strolling along the towpath to join us. I introduced him and they exchanged a few words before the lad made his way back to the village. We parted with my heartfelt good wishes for the life of adventure which I could see awaited him.

'Well, Watson,' said Holmes, as the lad departed. 'What have you learned?'

I told him what had passed between us and added that, in my opinion the lad's ambition should be encouraged, for he would make a fine soldier.

'His mother's name,' I continued, 'is Annie Bristow and they live in a small cottage at the opposite end of the village from Hanneford Hall. She seems to have a small income of some sort. There is no money to spare but they are not desperately poor.'

'When did they move to the village?'

'That I did not ask him.'

'A pity,' said Holmes, 'since it was the only matter of interest on which I was not already informed.'

'I did my best, Holmes,' I replied, rather stiffly.

'Of course. Well, the occasion was not entirely wasted. At least I was able to see the lad for myself, which was my object in meeting you here.'

'There is something more,' I said. "I told him a recruitin*g officer would ask for his date and place of birth. He is sixteen and was born at Kandahar on the 10th of March 1877.'

'Watson, my dear fellow, you excel yourself!' said Holmes. 'That indeed is information of the first importance. Now I must wire Cheffington tonight, for I shall need his help before we can proceed any further.' So saying, he sat down on the grass beside me, lit his pipe, and gave himself over to silent contemplation of the river. I knew that in this frame of mind it would be useless to ask him any questions so I wound in my tackle, threw my head back on the grass and enjoyed a pleasant doze in the afternoon sun.

*　　*　　*

We had not long to wait for Cheffington's reply. His wire came shortly before breakfast, two days later. It simply said—

Birth and marriage registered. H. has never been abroad. Arriving ten tomorrow.

He was true to his word and, in spite of himself, as I thought, flushed with excitement when we met at the station.

'Do you really think, Mr Holmes,' he said, 'that we shall get to the bottom of this business.'

'This is a hunting county, Mr Cheffington,' said Holmes, 'and this morning I hope we shall flush out our fox.'

We stepped into the waiting room for a few minutes, where Cheffington showed us the documents he had brought with him; documents which, at that stage, left

me none the wiser. Then we set off together for Hanneford Hall. As we approached the old house in daylight I
was struck by its neglected appearance. The window
frames were sadly in need of paint, ivy was growing up
the walls, and here and there the rendering was crumb-
ling away from the brickwork.

Our knock was answered by a cheerful, middle-aged
woman. 'Good morning, Mrs Price,' said Holmes. 'Have
the goodness to tell Sir Archie Hanneford that Mr Cheffington and two friends are here.'

She bustled off, with a puzzled expression on her face,
and a moment later showed us into a large study or
library where the baronet was seated at his desk. There
was a musty smell in the room. I noticed the ceiling
plaster was heavily cracked and there were patches of
damp on the walls. Hanneford rose as we entered, saying,
with some indignation, 'Good Lord, Cheffington! What
is the meaning of this?'

This was my first sight of the man. His beard was full
and his eyeglass dangled on its cord. But what caught my
attention at once were the same delicate features and
bright blue eyes that I had seen on young Sam Bristow.

It was Holmes who answered him. 'I am a consulting
detective," he said, "and Dr Watson here is my colleague.
I regret that Mr Cheffington has been put to the trouble
and expense of engaging our services in order to recover
a valuable book which you have purloined from the
College of Arms.'

'I have done nothing of the sort!' protested Hanneford.

'No bluster, please,' said Holmes, calmly taking out his

watch. 'If the book is not in my hands within two minutes I shall send for a constable.'

There was a moment's silence while Holmes stood, immobile, watch in hand and Hanneford looked from one to the other, his colour rising, and his features contorted as he struggled to contain his emotions. When he spoke, his voice was hardly under control.

'Damn you, Cheffington!' He said, 'I never meant to keep the thing. It's a family heirloom, and ought to be mine by rights. I only borrowed it for a week or two and then, when you made such a fuss, you put me in an impossible position. It's upstairs in my dressing room. I'll bring it down.'

He strode out of the room and we waited in silence for what seemed a very long interval before he returned, with the book in his hand. He offered it to Cheffington, but Holmes reached out and took it himself, and, walking towards the window, began to study it.

'Now, gentlemen,' said Hanneford, standing by the door of the room, 'I must ask you to leave. Cheffington, I trust that you will never again call on me without an invitation. You are no longer welcome in this house.'

But none of us made a move. I looked towards Holmes, who had taken out his lens and was closely studying the last few pages in the book, holding them up to the light from the window. At a nod from him I closed the door again, and he turned towards us.

'The game's up, Hanneford,' he said. 'I am looking at the most recent addendum to this invaluable family history. It was written, I suppose, by your late father?'

'Just so,' said Hanneford, with a note of caution in his voice.

'He records,' Holmes continued, 'his marriage to your mother, and the birth of two sons; yourself, of course, and your elder brother Jack, two years your senior. I assume that he, in the ordinary way, would have inherited your father's title?'

'Had he lived,' said Hanneford.

'Indeed. But against his name are written the words, *Died without issue.*'

'Sadly, that was the case, and so the title passed to me.'

'I am curious as to why you added that significant phrase, in your own hand, just a short while ago, when you collected the book from your dressing room.'

'I did nothing of the sort. That memorandum was added some time ago, when I learned of my brother's untimely death.'

'And yet the ink is still fresh. This is vellum, not paper. The surface is smooth and the ink will not harden for a day or two. Would you care to examine it through my lens?'

'Well what of it?' barked Hanneford. 'You are not suggesting the entry is false?'

'I do not know what has become of your elder brother. But his son and heir – the lawful heir to your father's title and estate – is alive and well. You know him, and you have cheated him of his inheritance.'

'Preposterous!'

'If you say so, the law must take its course. But I must warn you that you stand in very great peril. Better by far,

Hanneford, to lay the facts before me, in their entirety, so that I can decide how best to proceed.'

All this time Cheffington, whilst listening intently to the conversation, had said nothing. Now I thought he was about to intervene, when there was a knock at the door and Mrs Price announced that a Mrs Bristow had arrived.

'Who the devil is Mrs Bristow?' asked Hanneford. 'I have no business with her.'

'She comes here at my invitation,' said Holmes, 'and I strongly recommend that you receive her civilly.'

There was something in the tone of his voice which brooked no argument, and Hanneford subsided, while young Sam's mother was shown in. I have seen many handsome women in my time, but few to compare with the dark-skinned beauty who now stood before us. Tall, slender and erect, with a flawless complexion and dark, intelligent eyes, she glanced from one to the other as she waited to hear what we had to say.

Holmes introduced the four of us and begged her to take a seat.

'Is this about my son?' she asked, quietly. 'I hope he has not been troublesome.'

'Quite the contrary,' I said. 'I met him a few days ago. He is a fine boy and a credit to his mother. A mother who he told me,' I said, with a raise of one eyebrow, was an Indian princess.'

'I am a Sikh,' she said. 'In our religion every man is Singh, a lion, and every woman is Kaur, a princess. I am Anand Kaur. So,' she added, with a ghost of a smile and a slight inclination of her head, 'perhaps he may call me a princess.'

At that, Hanneford gave a half-suppressed, scornful laugh.

'Be silent!' said Holmes, with a sudden asperity, and then turning to Mrs Bristow, addressed her as follows—

'I have asked you here to tell us what you know of your husband, and what has become of him. It is, I assure you, a matter of some importance, and may be very much to your own advantage, and that of your son. But only if you tell us the plain truth, and the whole truth. There must be no romancing. Do I make myself clear?'

'If I am willing to tell you, will you be telling my son?'

'That remains to be seen. We have only the boy's interests at heart. However, we must have the facts, if you please.'

There was a long pause, while the lady collected her thoughts, and then she began.

'My husband was Jack Bristow. He was a British soldier with the mountain guns, the little guns which they carry on the backs of mules. He was a farrier, not a gunner. It was his job to shoe the mules. We met when he was in India, in the garrison. We were married and we had a baby boy.'

'Some barrack room, jump over the broomstick affair, I suppose,' said Hanneford.

'No,' she said, quietly. 'It was a proper wedding with the chaplain. The officer permitted it and so did my brothers, so all was correct.'

'And as Cheffington, here, has discovered,' said Holmes,

'the marriage was duly registered and your son was born in lawful wedlock. Pray continue.'

'Soon after the baby came we had very bad luck. My husband was kicked by a mule. It was a very bad wound, a blow to the head. After that, he could not talk properly. He made sudden noises, and he was drinking too much, so they sent him back to England. And because we had a proper wedding, they let me go with him, and the baby.'

'Where did you go?' asked Holmes.

'To the barracks at Woolwich. But it was not good, because Jack was always drinking. He used to go away for a few days. When he came back they would lock him up and then he would go away again. And one day he went away and never came back.'

'How did you manage?' I asked.

'It was very hard, because I had no money. I worked in the laundry, and sometimes some of the soldiers helped me a little. When I was ill, for a few weeks, we went into the workhouse. Then one day the chaplain came and said, the officers had found some money for me, and a place to live, because they knew my husband had been a good soldier before he was injured. So they sent me and the baby down here, and found me the cottage, and every week they send me a little money.'

'Your son told Dr Watson," said Holmes, "that his father was the son of a nobleman, enlisted under an assumed name.'

'Jack told me that once, when he was in drink, but he told me many foolish things. I did not believe him.'

'Yet you told your son, who does believe it.'

'I want my son to be proud of his father.'

'Very well,' said Holmes. 'And now, Hanneford, we shall hear your side of the story. Tell us nothing but the truth.'

Hanneford shrugged and said, 'Since you insist on meddling in my affairs, you shall know the truth, for there is very little to hide.

'When I was a boy I worshipped my elder brother, Jack. But he was a madcap, daredevil kind of fellow and at eighteen he ran away from home. As I later learned, he enlisted in the Artillery at Woolwich. He knew that if our father discovered him there he would be purchased out, so he enlisted under a false name.

'Within weeks he sailed for India, and was sent to the North West Frontier. He was a poor correspondent. He wrote but once a year, on Christmas day, a single line to say that he was fit and well. He had to put his name and military unit on the back of the envelope, which is how my parents learned he had adopted the name Bristow and was serving in Afghanistan. But by then it was too late for my father to intervene.

'The letters came every year, once a year, and always just the same message. "I am fit and well." The last was in 1877. The next year there was nothing. Alarmed, my father wrote to the War Office. But as you will know, Cheffington, the War Office has its own strict procedures. If you wish to enquire about a serving soldier you must complete a special form, and your signature must be witnessed by a clergyman or churchwarden. When the form is returned to you, a few weeks later, it contains

only the barest information. In Jack's case it simply said:
Deserted 29th November 1878.

'My father had closely followed the campaigns on the North West Frontier, and in Afghanistan, studying the artists' views in the Graphic. For him, the date had a terrible significance, for on that day the mountain guns were in action at the battle of Peiwar Kotal. The implication was clear. Jack had deserted his comrades under fire.

'My father's shame and anger were terrible. I can see him now, in this very room, declaring that Jack's name was never again to be mentioned in this house. My mother wept bitterly, but my father was not to be moved.

'It was a heavy blow. My father was not a young man and not in the best of health. Within five years he succumbed to a disease of the heart. We never heard from Jack again and I had no idea that he was married, still less that he had a son. So I naturally inherited my father's title as the tenth baronet.

'My mother lived in this house for another ten years. I lived in London, with Mrs Price as my housekeeper. Then last year, when my mother was dying, I learned the truth about Jack for the first time.

'She told me that after my father's death she had travelled to Woolwich. Not for her the War Office forms and official procedures. She was determined to find out for herself exactly what had become of her son. She saw the regimental chaplain, who by good chance had known Jack, and thought well of him. It turned out, as you have heard, that he had not deserted his comrades on the battlefield. He had been injured behind the lines and shipped home from India two or three years earlier. Before his accident he had been well regarded in the regiment, but after his injury he went downhill and took to drink.

'From time to time he would go absent without leave. When he returned to barracks he was disciplined. But his last absence lasted for some weeks. Eventually, when he had been missing for three months he was posted as a deserter. The date, by pure coincidence, was also the date of a battle many hundreds of miles away, in which he had no part.

'From the chaplain also, my mother learned that Jack had been married in India and had left a widow and a young son. The widow was this woman, of course, who seemed to be living from hand to mouth, and the son was her half-caste boy. My mother understood only too well that if the marriage was recognised the boy would be the true heir to my father's title, as the son of the eldest son.

'All this my mother kept to herself, for she had no intention of disinheriting me. At the same time, she could not see her grandson starve. So, without a word to me, she found them a cottage at the other end of the village and made them a small allowance. My mother took an interest in the boy's progress, of course, but always at a distance, never hinting at any special connection. All this was arranged through the regimental chaplain at Woolwich. To preserve her secret my mother asked him to say, that the money had been provided by subscription from the officers and sergeants.'

'I believed it,' said Mrs Bristow. 'Until this minute I believed it.'

'And I knew nothing of it, at the time,' said Hanneford. 'As I say, it was only at my mother's death bed that I learned the truth.'

'Nor did I know my husband's true name. But now I know and I see that my son has been cheated.'

'Your son, and your husband also, if by any chance he is still alive,' said Holmes.

'Jack was drowned. They found his body one morning in the Surrey Commercial Docks. It was a year or more after he went missing. The boy has not been told, and I do not wish to tell him. I told him his father died in battle.'

'Oh, if the truth is to come out, it must all come out,' said Hanneford.

'Hanneford!' cried Cheffington, 'this is unworthy of you.'

'And most unwise,' said Holmes, 'considering that just a short while ago you attempted to deceive us by uttering a forged document, for which I believe the penalty is up to fourteen years in the second division. But let us complete the story. On your mother's death you took up residence here and at the first opportunity made it your business to take a look at your nephew. To your dismay, young as he was, he bore a remarkable resemblance to yourself. That was not something to which you wished to draw attention, which accounts for your decision to grow a beard and purchase an eyeglass.'

'All this over a wretched book!' said Hanneford. 'I suppose the last entry was irregular. I admit it, but I have nothing to be ashamed of. When Jack changed his name and deserted his regiment he broke my father's heart. He had no further claim on this family. He forfeited the title.'

'My husband was a good soldier,' said Mrs Bristow, 'and a very good man until the mule kicked him.'

'What I cannot understand,' said Cheffington, 'is why you took the book in the first place. If you simply wanted to make another entry, why not do that in the library, with the librarian's permission?'

'That was my first idea,' said Hanneford. 'But when I saw the old book again I reflected what a fine manuscript it was. Even the few short entries made by my father were impeccable for he was a fine penman. I knew that I should make a poor fist of anything I wrote, especially if my hand was nervous. Then it occurred to me that it might be possible to find a law clerk, or someone with a good hand who knew how to write on vellum, to make the entries for me. So on the spur of the moment, when the librarian was distracted, I put the book under my coat and came away.

'When I got the book home, I realised that sooner or later it would be missed, and that smuggling it back into the library might be more difficult than smuggling it out. In short, I was at a loss, and to tell you the truth, my nerve failed me. So I simply left the book on the table in my room and did nothing. When you wrote to me, Cheffington, after your visit, I was still undecided what to do, but I did not care to admit that I had taken the book, so I took refuge in silence.'

'I do not mind about an old leather book,' said Mrs Bristow, who had seen what Holmes was holding. 'What I mind about is my son and how he has been cheated.'

'I suppose I have Mrs Price and her wagging tongue to thank for this,' said Hanneford. 'I should have dismissed her weeks ago.'

'Possibly so,' said Holmes, 'since her wages are now five months in arrears.'

'Damn your impertinence!' said Hanneford, flushing a vivid scarlet.

'Mrs Price has indeed been of great assistance,' said Holmes, 'but I can assure you she is quite without malice and means you no harm. By the way, Cheffington,' he continued, 'you have established that the house goes with the title, and that both devolve to the heir-at-law?'

'The house is held in trust for the tenth baronet,' said Cheffington, 'whoever that may be.'

'However,' Holmes continued, 'as we see from the condition of this room the place is sadly in need of repair. I think, Hanneford, for all your ancient title, you are not a wealthy man?'

'That is none of your business, Holmes! At least I have kept up Mrs Bristow's allowance, for which she should be grateful.'

'As to that,' said Holmes, 'we shall see, for I think it is time to bring this unhappy affair to a conclusion. Mrs Bristow, will you be content if your son takes the title which is rightly his and you are secured a modest increase in your weekly allowance? Strictly speaking, your son is also entitled to the house but that, I think, would be a very troublesome inheritance.'

'I want only what is best for Sam.'

'Watson, how much was your wound pension when you came back from Afghanistan?'

'Eleven shillings and sixpence a day, Holmes.'

'Well, for the mother and son together, let us round it up to five guineas a week. Will you undertake to pay that sum, Hanneford, for your nephew and his mother, and let them continue in the cottage?'

'Have I no choice in the matter?'

'Practically speaking, none.'

'And will you keep silent,' I asked, 'about the boy's father and how he met his death.'

'Very well.'

'And I must formally ask you,' said Cheffington, 'as required by law, to discontinue the style and title of baronet.'

Before he could answer, Mrs Bristow had risen to her feet. Her eyes were bright, but once again, she spoke quietly.

'No,' she said, 'this is not right. We were very poor and without his mother's help we should have starved. Also, the money has come every week since she died. Anyway, my son is too young for everyone to call him "Sir". Let Mr Hanneford be the baronet for the time being. Then, when Sam is 21, he can be the baronet.'

'A very generous offer, in my view,' I said.

Hanneford closed his eyes for a moment and muttered,

'Ridiculous!'

'Ridiculous indeed,' said Cheffington, 'considered strictly as a matter of law. But I can see no objection to an informal arrangement along those lines. The hurried entry you made in this book, Hanneford, can be erased and replaced by a brief statement of the facts which have now come to light. There need be nothing stated to your discredit.'

So, in a few minutes, all was agreed. But before we left Holmes found Mrs Price, took her to one side and, with that charm which he could always employ when the occasion required, persuaded her to say nothing of our visit.

*   *   *

'You must tell us your chain of reasoning, Holmes,' I said, as we sat with Cheffington in our railway carriage on the journey back to London, with the precious old book safely secured in his portfolio.

'At first,' said Holmes, 'I had little to work on, beyond the obvious fact that Hanneford had something to conceal and that his secret was somehow connected to his family's history, and his own facial appearance. He was evidently nervous and awkward, Cheffington, from the moment you first appeared on his doorstep. He knew that he had purloined a book from the library and did not know whether you had yet discovered the loss. As the minutes passed and no mention was made of the book, his fears receded and he invited you to lunch. He could not show you over the house, of course, lest you catch sight of the book in his dressing room. Then Mrs Price arrived and suggested a visit to the beehives and a confidential talk.

'That was too much for Hanneford. A man who dislikes bees, as she told you he did, must stay away from beehives. But if Mrs Price and yourself were left to talk in the garden he could not know what topics you might touch upon. Doubtless she would have noticed the curious old book in his dressing room and, knowing your interest in such things, she might have mentioned it. In any case, a private conversation between a housekeeper who knew something of his private affairs and a gentleman well versed in the laws of descent and inheritance, was not to be countenanced. He took fright, and practically ordered you out of the house.

'Before we left for Castle Acre I consulted *Burke* and *Debrett*. Both are full of medieval nonsense but fairly sound for the present century. Both had entries for Hanneford but, as is often the case, neither was up to date. *Burke* still showed the title vested in the father, the 9th baronet, with no record of his death. *Debrett* was much the same. But both recorded the birth of two sons, a significant piece of information for it showed that your friend Archibald was the younger son.

'When we arrived in the village my first task, as you know, was to befriend Mrs Price. From her I learned something about bees and rather more about her neighbours. The young lad who wished to enlist and was said to be the son of a nobleman seemed worthy of further investigation, which is why I put him in your way,

Watson.

'I also learned that Hanneford was in the habit of taking an early morning walk, which was generally the only time he left the house. The next morning I followed his example. When our paths crossed, as I made sure they did, I had a good view of his features.

'By the time we met young Sam on the river bank I had paid Mrs Price a second visit and made her a present of my *Langstroth*. Then it was that she confided the true state of her employer's financial affairs.

'Until then I had been feeling my way. But as soon as I saw the lad's face I perceived the likeness to Hanneford; a strong family resemblance, beyond doubt. My first thought, of course, was that the boy might be his natural son. However if Sam was born in India, as Mrs Price had told me, and if Hanneford had never been in that country, that left only one other possibility.

'The boy's date of birth, which you found out, Watson, was invaluable. That evening I wired Cheffington with my suggestions and he was able to further our enquiries.'

'The Army keeps a record of regimental births, deaths and marriages overseas,' said Cheffington 'and the registers are kept at Somerset House. It was the work of a few minutes to find the entry for Sam's birth and but a few minutes more to find the entry for his parent's marriage. I knew that Hanneford had never been abroad for we had spoken about that in the past. That was the information I wired to you, Mr Holmes.

'It took me a little longer to trace the father's will but that was also at Somerset House. There was no mention of either son, as he left the whole estate to his widow. I searched for her will and found there was none. She died intestate, so the house passed, with the title, to the heir at law.

'The hardest task was my search for any record of Jack Hanneford. I found his birth, of course, but from then to the present time no trace of his death, or indeed a marriage.'

'And of course none will be found,' said Holmes. 'I was now convinced that Hanneford's keeping to the house, except in the early morning, the beard and the eyeglass, were all part of a design. He wanted no inquisitive villagers to compare his features with those of Sam Bristow. No doubt this occasioned some inconvenience, but he had every hope that the boy would soon enlist, and then the danger would be past.

'I still had no proof that the boy was his nephew. Of one thing, however, I was perfectly convinced. He had stolen the book, for who else could have taken it and for what purpose? I decided to drive home my advantage and confront the man with his brother's widow. The rest you know. His bungled attempt at a last-minute forgery played into my hands.'

'And what of the entries in *Burke* and *Debrett*?' I asked.

'That he could easily have dealt with. He had only to drop a line to the editors, intimating that his elder brother had died without issue, and they would have corrected the entry in the next edition.'

'You have your brother to thank for this adventure,' I said, 'but I should like to know what he meant by the cryptic formula at the foot of his letter.'

'This is art, not algebra,' said Holmes with a smile, taking the letter from his inside pocket. The q is an eye-glass with its dangling cord and the v is a beard. It was the combination of the two, designed to alter Hanne-ford's appearance, which aroused Mycroft's suspicions and persuaded him that the case was worth looking into. Indeed he was probably half way to solving the mystery before you, Cheffington, stepped over our threshold.'

*　　*　　*

A few weeks later Holmes and I were guests of the Earl Marshal at the annual ceremony at the College of Arms. I am sure that when the question was put to the Bar the Honourable Rupert Cheffington, Bluemantle Pursuivant of Arms, made his bow with a particular satisfaction. It is pleasing to report, that in due course he was elevated to the rank of Somerset Herald and in that capacity atten-ded the coronations of the both the present king and his late father.

Archie Hanneford Esq (formerly known as Sir Archi-bald Hanneford, Bart) did not survive the great influenza epidemic of 1918. He died in straightened circumstan-ces, having sold Hanneford Hall to pay his debts. To his credit, however, he kept up Mrs Bristow's allowance till the end.

Sir Samrath Hanneford Bart, having served with distin-ction in the Great War, is now the senior Band Sergeant Major at the Royal Military School of Music at Kneller Hall, where his mother, affectionately known as 'The

Princess' is a frequent and well-respected visitor.

My readers will recall that since his retirement to the South Coast Sherlock Holmes has become an enthusiastic beekeeper.

THE PHANTOM GUN HORSE

I MET Sherlock Holmes on two occasions. We had a family connection, of sorts. My mother's sister, Phoebe, married a widower, Dr John Watson: the same Dr Watson who was Holmes's friend and colleague for many years, and wrote up his cases for The Strand Magazine.

Of our first meeting I have only a dim recollection, as I was only a youngster at the time. My mother and her sister had taken a cottage at Hove for a week and one afternoon we drove over to Fulworth to call on Holmes in his retirement cottage. The great detective was then in his early seventies but still in good health, and with a keen eye. He asked about my puppy dog, and showed me his beehives before I went off to play on the cliffs for an hour or so.

Our next meeting was many years later, in the anxious days of 1943. I was in uniform, working on our top secret plans for the invasion of Normandy. Uncle John had died, naming me as one of his executors and leaving Holmes the famous 'battered tin dispatch box' in which he kept his records of the cases on which they had worked together. This box I had to take down to Fulworth.

Holmes was now very old and the years of heavy smoking had taken their toll. He had a troublesome cough, his eyes were rheumy and he walked with a stick. But his mind was as sharp as ever.

He was delighted to receive the dispatch box, only regretting that he had not seen more of 'Good old Watson' in recent years. We opened it in his study. It was full to overflowing with neatly labelled packets of documents. Most of these comprised medical and business correspondence from the 1920s but included among them I was delighted to find the manuscripts of the six stories here published for the first time. They had been carefully revised, in my uncle's very neat and legible hand and I was able to read some extracts to Holmes. As he listened he nodded and smiled occasionally breaking in to say, 'Quite correct' or 'Yes, I had forgotten that detail.'

I naturally asked whether there could be any objection to my submitting these stories to a publisher to which the great detective simply replied, 'Wait till I'm gone. It won't matter then.' Why they had not been published in my uncle's lifetime I do not know. It may be that they took second place to his interest in ophthalmology on which he did some valuable work in his later years and for which indeed he was awarded the MBE shortly before his death.

I must mention two more items which we found in the dispatch box. One, carefully wrapped in linen and tied with pink tape, was the small casket which features in the adventure of the Ottoman Saloon, to which I must refer my readers. The other was a sheet of blue notepaper, on which Uncle John had simply written 'The Phantom Gun Horse.' When I asked Holmes whether this was a case which he remembered he gave a dry chuckle.

'Dear Boy, your uncle's accounts of my cases were always scrupulously accurate. However, from time to time he would throw in a reference to some other case for which "the public was not yet ready", or some such nonsense. He might mention, for example, The Giant Rat of Sumatra or The Singular Affair of the Aluminium Crutch. Now some of those references, I regret to say, were entirely fictitious. To my chagrin they were included merely to intrigue and excite the reader's curiosity. It was a mildly disreputable practice, to which, indeed, I more than once objected, and I fear that The Phantom Gun Horse is one such fiction. To my knowledge there never was such a case. It is merely an example of dear old Watson's artistic licence, for which I suppose I shall have to forgive him.'

MK
Whitsun, 1987

ABOUT THE AUTHOR

Malcolm Knott is a retired barrister who sat for many years as a Recorder in the London Crown Courts. He lives in Suffolk and collects postage stamps, brass weights and toy soldiers.

Printed in Great Britain
by Amazon

53679550R00127